MARDI GRAS AND MAGIC

THE WITCHES OF THE FRENCH QUARTER

JEN PITTS

*For All My Family
Those Lost and Those Found*

CONTENTS

1

The day I buried my mother, I discovered I was a witch.

Technically, I didn't bury her since she insisted on being cremated. And I wasn't a witch. Not yet, at least, according to Luella Leblanc from the Fontenot Coven. To claim my birthright, I needed to bring my mother's ashes to her birthplace, New Orleans.

"Althea, your momma hid the truth from you, but it's time to bring you out of the darkness. Fern should have done it herself, but it's too late now," Luella said.

She must be joking. I wanted to head back to my hotel, kick off my stiff high heels, strip off this scratchy black dress, and pour myself a glass of Chardonnay. Instead, I sat on the edge of an uncomfortable plastic chair in the Reflections room of the Evergreen Funeral Home in Seattle. Before I could leave with my mother's urn, this stranger rushed into the room. She sat next to me, introduced herself as a friend of my mother's, and began the strangest conversation I'd ever had.

I played along. She appeared harmless, at least physically. Two-inch-high sensible black pumps made her five feet tall, and the long, black wool coat covered her lean body. But the intensity of her stare made me squirm as if I had been called into the school principal's office.

"I'm sorry, but you must have my mother confused with someone else. Fern Fontenot owned a plant nursery, played cribbage every other Tuesday, and made the best chocolate chip cookies. She most definitely was not a witch in a coven with her last name."

"That's who she became after she left the French Quarter. But she is—was… " I heard a catch in her throat, but she regained her composure. "Your momma was a powerful witch. She hid it from you, but that doesn't mean it isn't true. When you're in New Orleans, you'll discover her truth and yours."

"New Orleans? My mother and I haven't been there since we left when I was six."

"Goodness, you don't know about Fern's yearly visits to your family home?" Luella shook her head. "I hoped she had at least told you about Fontenot Mansion. It's your responsibility now."

I shivered even as stale, warm air filled the room from the vents. I wanted to tell this lady she was wrong, but I couldn't. Her insistent manner didn't convince me. She wore a silver locket embossed with a star jasmine on the front. It matched the one my mother had worn except Luella's was on a short chain. My mother's locket hung from a long chain, and she hid the necklace under her shirt most days. My mother insisted the jewelry was ordinary, and the jasmine on the front and the dried jasmine inside lacked any significance. But why would she have her last name engraved on the back of the necklace if it wasn't important?

The necklace sat at the bottom of my purse since I hadn't decided what to do with it. I didn't believe that the necklace was an ordinary one; my mother kept it close to her until the day she died. I hesitated to wear it as it felt heavy in my hands. There was also an emotional weight to it I didn't want to feel right now.

My heart told me I needed to listen to Luella. But my head tried to fight back.

"I can't just jump on a plane with a total stranger and go to a house I supposedly own."

"Yes, you can, and yes, you will. The coven needs you, and by the looks of it, you need us."

"What's that supposed to mean?"

"Child, you're sitting by yourself at your momma's funeral. You're exhausted, confused, and alone. Your life is going nowhere. That's what you're thinking."

"I'm alone because the service is over. Yes, I'm exhausted after dealing with my mother's death. And you don't know what I'm thinking."

But she did. The sudden death of my mother left me full of confusion and regret. We hadn't been close, but it wasn't for a lack of trying on my part. My mother forbade any talk of her past. As much as I tried, my mom always said, "The past is the past. Look toward your future."

That's what she did. She never talked about her family, her life, or even my father. She created a life for us in Seattle. And now she was dead, and even after rooting through her house like a child looking for Christmas gifts, I found nothing.

Then again, my home wouldn't say much about me either if I died today. As of tomorrow, I wouldn't own a house. I stowed away what little possessions I had in a storage locker except for two suitcases of the things I deemed necessary. My flight to Australia left in two weeks, taking me to my daughter.

The one thing I had done right in my life was my daughter, Olivia. Our relationship was the opposite of mine and my mother's. I gave birth to her when I was twenty, so we grew up together in many ways. She was now twenty-six and exploring the world. Her adventurous nature, confidence, and bravery were qualities I admired in her and wished I had.

"I'll tell you how you're feeling. You're angry at the driver who hit your momma and left her for dead right in front of her home. That anger is nothing compared to the pain and resentment you have for your momma. You're worried you'll never know who she really was, and in turn, you won't know who you are."

I glared at the woman, wanting to shout that she was wrong. But I couldn't. For my entire life, my mother had been a closed book. No matter how much I asked about my past and my father, she never disclosed her secrets. I assumed she took her past and mine with her to her grave. Yet this stranger said I could have all the answers.

"So let me get this straight." I took in a deep breath. "My mom was a witch and now I'm a witch. Can I cast spells? Do I need to dance around a fire while chanting naked?" My patience had worn thin. Maybe this woman went around to funerals, making these strange statements as a cruel joke.

"Don't be flippant, young lady." Luella pulled her black leather gloves off and rubbed her hands together. "Witches must take their responsibility with the utmost care. But yes, you will do spells. How do you think you and your daughter have that beautiful hair? Your momma put spells on you so you'd have that blonde hair for your whole life. No gray hair for any Fontenot women."

I twisted a strand of my hair, a habit my mother had tried to break me of. Hairstylists never believed me when I insisted my hair was natural. My mother didn't have one gray hair, and I assumed it was genetics, not magic.

"Thea, Fern Marguerite Fontenot hid everything from you, trying to keep you safe. Your lack of knowledge of your gifts hurts you now. I insisted she tell you the truth. She agreed to write a letter in case something happened to her, but I doubt it's the entire story."

"And you're going to tell me the rest of the story?"

"In a minute, a lawyer will hand you that letter." Luella pointed her closed black umbrella at the entrance to the viewing room. The sound of footsteps on the polished wood floor made me jump. A man in a navy-blue suit, carrying a briefcase headed toward us.

"Do you know what my mother wrote?"

"No. Fern's magic was powerful and even I can't break the spell here. What I will tell you is that after you read that letter, we're going to New Orleans. You need to know who you are, so you can find your momma's killer and save the coven."

2

———

My mother's letter didn't tell the entire story. My mother had explained I now owned the deteriorating family home in the French Quarter. It was held in a trust, and the lawyer would handle the sale. Any profit would be split between me and Olivia. She ended the letter with, "Don't go to the house. Let the lawyers handle it. It's our past and not your future. I mean it. Please trust me."

My mother didn't know me well. Who wouldn't go to a secret family home and see it for themselves? When I showed the letter to Luella, she cackled so loudly that the funeral home director rushed into the room. "She's just overwhelmed by my mother's death," I said, so the director left us alone.

"Your momma is a bald-faced liar. The house isn't run down. I've taken care of it as if it were my own. It's where our coven has met for over one hundred years. We need it, and you do too."

Luella's reason for visiting became crystal clear. She

wanted the house as a free place for her witches. What kind of con was this?

"Child, you're wrong. I'm not a con artist looking for a free place for us."

I didn't respond, not that I needed to since, apparently, Luella read minds.

Luella's laugh lines deepened as she grinned. "Yes, I read your mind. It's something we're both capable of doing. We need to fix that and so much more."

I stared at Luella like she had sprouted a third eye. How could ESP be real? My heart raced at the thought of this stranger digging into my head. I bit the inside of my lip to focus on that pain so I wouldn't think of anything else.

"Fix me? Are you comparing me to a broken-down car?" I rubbed the back of my neck, feeling all of my forty-six years.

"Goodness, you make the same sourpuss face as your momma. All I'm saying is you have a lot to learn."

A week later, I was sitting in the back of a taxi on my way to learn the truth. I verified our family had a home in New Orleans, but I found no evidence that my mother had supernatural powers. Luella was going to have a hard time persuading me I came from a line of witches.

I had no idea what to expect, which made me very uncomfortable. My daughter teased me about my excessive planning tendencies, but I couldn't change my behavior no matter how I tried. Taking this trip was the most spontaneous thing I'd ever done.

As soon as the cab entered the French Quarter, my worries momentarily disappeared. The explosion of colors was a shock to my system. Sunny yellow, cheerful green, soft pink, and vibrant teal were just a few of the unique color combinations on the shotgun cottages. Before I left Seattle. I researched New Orleans architecture and learned about the cottages and the brick town houses with intricate wrought-iron balconies. As if the houses themselves weren't special on their own, the added embellishments made me smile. Decorations of purple, green, and gold must be for Mardi Gras season. Fleur-de-lis flags, wreaths wrapped in ribbons, and even plastic skeletons wearing beads added a sense of playfulness to the homes.

I opened the window of the taxi, letting the warm air and sun take away the chills that ran through me as we turned on to Burgundy Street. My first view of my family home in forty years was coming up.

My mother and I moved away from New Orleans when I was six. I didn't remember my time here. Perhaps it was normal, but the way Luella looked at me when I said I remembered nothing made me think otherwise. Could my mother have hypnotized me to erase those memories? I didn't bother to ask Luella because her answer for every-thing was, "Your mother was a witch."

"You must be a tourist." The taxi driver and I made eye contact in his rearview mirror. "Only out-of-towners love the warm weather in February."

"I just left two inches of snow so this feels like heaven." I laughed. "Is it always this warm in the winter?"

"It can get cold, too. But no snow unless a Voodoo queen decides we need it."

"I guess I better not make enemies with a queen, then." The cab came to a sudden stop and my knees hit the back of the front seat.

"If you're going in there, you definitely don't want to mess with Voodoo people." He pointed at the house where we stopped. "Are you sure this is the right address? Only witches go in there."

"This house is for witches?" My voice went up an octave.

"Honey, everyone in the neighborhood knows this place." He turned and faced me, his wide eyes staring at me as if I had horns growing out of my head. "I've never seen you before, though. Are you a new one?"

"A new what?"

"A witch, of course! If not, let me take you to a nice hotel, and you can enjoy your vacation. Someone must be playing tricks on you."

That's what I believed, too, but I had to figure out what to do with my family home. I refused to be distracted by all this talk of witches. I stepped out of the cab and waited on the sidewalk as the driver took my bags out of the trunk.

"Someone might be playing a trick, but I need to find out. Thank you." I paid the driver, who accepted my money without making eye contact and quickly took off in his car.

Time to find out the truth.

3

With two suitcases and a sense of foreboding, I stood on the sidewalk in front of Fontenot Mansion. Worry changed to amazement as I took in the house. The building was a four-story brick townhouse with a wrought-iron fence protecting a curved staircase and a large entry hall to the backyard. Or rather, courtyard, from what I gleaned reading about New Orleans architecture. The photos I looked at showed brightly colored cottages and brick townhouses, but it didn't prepare me for seeing my family home in person.

The curved staircase led to a landing with two windows and a large white door. Above the landing were two more floors with wrought-iron balconies and three windows, each with green shutters. The top floor appeared to be an attic with one dormer window.

The front door swung open and Luella stepped out. "Are you just going to stand there gawking? Do you remember your home?"

I shook my head. But something about this place settled

the butterflies in my stomach. Luella strode down the stairs and opened the gate to meet me on the sidewalk.

"You used to draw all over the sidewalk. When the rain washed away your pictures, you'd stomp your little feet." Luella's face softened as she spoke. "You used every color in that box of chalk to create your sidewalk garden."

"I'm not surprised. That's the only garden I can grow." I laughed.

"What do you mean? We're all good with plants and flowers." Luella stepped over to me, letting the gate swing shut behind her. Without her high heels, she came up to my shoulders, but her presence was still bigger than life.

"By 'we' do you mean witches?" I said.

The sense of nostalgia turned to annoyance. I needed to put this witch business aside and look at the house. I had an appointment with the lawyer about the family trust next week. He said he couldn't fit me in any earlier. Once I found out how to sell the house, I'd hire a real estate agent. The money would fund the next stage of my life—not that I had any actual plans after visiting Olivia. No responsibilities meant I could do as I wanted. In theory, it sounded exciting, but there was a sense of doubt that nagged at me.

One step at a time for now. And the next step was entering Fontenot Mansion.

"Welcome home, Althea." Luella closed the door behind us. I pulled my luggage into the first room off the hallway.

"You've taken great care of the place." The house was immaculate and furnished with an eclectic assortment of antiques and contemporary furniture. Although the couches had a modern appearance, the coffee table and chairs encircling it were Victorian style. Red and white roses filled crystal vases and porcelain urns. The yellow color palette made the room bright even with the floor-to-ceiling curtains closed on the front windows.

But there was no hint of anything personal. There were no photographs which I expected in a family home. By the patches of darker wallpaper and pinprick holes, I'd bet there had been paintings or photos on the walls.

The house reminded me of a showroom or museum. A chill lingered in the air. I searched the ceiling for vents, but found none.

"The air-conditioning works well in here," I said.

"The air-conditioning isn't on. Don't you know anything about ghosts?" Luella said.

"Ghosts? Sorry, I was too busy reading up on witches," I deadpanned.

"I highly doubt that, or you would have packed a magic wand." Luella turned her head as a large, orange tabby sauntered into the room. "Can you believe that, Tasso? This girl knows nothing."

"Aren't you a pretty kitty?" I crouched down and reached out to the plump cat with my hand. Growing up, my mother didn't allow pets. When I moved out on my own, I adopted a cat right away. My last fur baby, Agatha Christie-Cat, passed away a year ago, and I hadn't adopted another one.

"Go on, Tasso, say hello to Althea." A smile crept up on Luella's face as the cat strolled over to me.

Tasso sniffed my outstretched hand, and then I stroked his head. His soft fur was smooth under my hands. "Such a cute kitty. Did you get your name because you're plump like a sausage?"

"Don't fat-shame me because I like good food."

I fell backward, landing on my butt with my legs splayed

out. Did he speak? His mouth moved, and the words sounded as if they came from him.

Tasso flicked his tail back and forth while Luella's giggles reminded me of nails on a chalkboard. I pulled my legs into a criss-cross position, as I wasn't sure I could stand up. My face felt as warm as a wood-burning stove.

Tasso stopped whipping his tail, so I reached out and picked him up. He must weigh fifteen pounds, but I raised him up, looking for a battery compartment. The warm body and intense eyes made him look like an actual cat. When he hissed and scratched my hand, I didn't doubt he was real.

I dropped the cat. "Okay, Luella, stop laughing. Are all witches ventriloquists?" I blotted the blood with a tissue from my purse.

"It wasn't me! Cats can speak to witches. When they want to, of course." Luella sat on the couch where Tasso licked his paws to wash his face.

"Thea-Bea, you don't remember me, do you? We played together! You drew my outline on the sidewalk like I was dead." Tasso turned to Luella. "She remembers nothing? Does she even use her powers?"

Thea-Bea? My mom called me that, but no one else did. Or at least that's what I thought. Cats didn't live to be forty years old, did they? This couldn't be real.

"We've got to help Althea get her gifts back. Fern blocked them, but I can break the spells. So be patient with her." Luella brushed her hands on her skirt and stood up.

"Just don't call me fat and we'll be good, Thea-Bea." Tasso trotted to the doorway. "Let's go to the courtyard. The coven awaits."

My heart thumped in my chest and my ears buzzed. I had to follow a supposed witch and a talking cat to a court-yard where a coven waited for me.

"Do you need a forklift to get up?" Tasso meowed, and turned down the hallway.

"You'll be fine, Althea." Luella extended her hand to me. I grasped it, and she pulled me up in one swift move. Her slight physique hid a physical strength. Did witches do spells that strengthened you? I couldn't believe I was even entertaining the idea. What was happening to me?

4

Women from their early twenties to their late seventies stood in small groups around the enclosed courtyard. They weren't wearing pointy witch hats or long, black robes, but they all wore the same necklace as my mother's. Other than that, they appeared normal. If I didn't know any better, I'd say it was a PTA meeting or a garden club party.

The way they studied me made goose bumps pop up on my arms. Some gawked at me, their mouths hanging open and their eyes looking me up and down. Others sneered, whispering to one another in angry tones.

A woman in her early twenties stepped to the front of the group. Dressed in a short, black dress with stilettos, she looked ready to go to a nightclub. Her stylish haircut and her makeup, in shades of pink, added to her polished look. Her laser-focused eyes never left me as she tightened the grip on her designer pink handbag. While the others weren't welcoming, they didn't display the anger that she did.

A light breeze came through the courtyard. The fragrant

scent of jasmine from the vines draped over the surrounding brick walls lulled me into a temporary state of calm. The sound of cascading water from a three-tier water fountain reminded me of the ones my mother had sold in her nursery. I wanted to take off my shoes to feel the cool slate under my feet. There was something comforting about the courtyard. Was this déjà vu, or was I looking for solace during this absurd moment?

Whatever it was, it vanished when the young woman stormed toward me. "Your mother was a killer!"

The only sound I heard was the beating of my heart. All eyes were on me as the room fell silent.

"Chloe, stop your foolishness! I've told you time and time again, Fern was no murderer." Luella stepped in between me and the woman.

"My momma said otherwise. Two witches, including my grandmother, died at the hands of a Fontenot witch. She doesn't deserve to be here," Chloe said.

I wanted to grab Luella by the arm and demand an explanation. She said my mother was murdered, not that she was a murderer. But first, I had to deal with Chloe. I stood up tall and looked into Chloe's eyes.

"My name is Althea Fontenot, and I am now the legal owner of this home. For a group that wants to keep using this place, you have some nerve calling my mother a killer."

"You may own it legally, but our coven has been here for over a hundred years. We're stronger than any piece of paper you can throw at us," Chloe said.

"Let's all calm down." Luella cleared her throat. "Althea just lost her mother, and if you'll recall, she doesn't have her powers right now. We need to introduce her back into the fold."

Tasso rubbed up against my legs and then sat next to

me. "Thea-Bea, don't you listen to cranky Chloe. She thinks she's the queen bee, but she's just another gator from the bayou."

"Shut your mouth, you mangy mutt," Chloe snapped.

"You can't even insult me correctly," Tasso meowed.

A spattering of giggles stopped when Chloe whipped her head around to the group. She faced me again, leaning over Luella's shoulder. "Whatever, fat cat. Listen, Althea, I've been a witch all my life. I'm from a good family and I'm the future of this coven. Give us the house, and go back to your basic life."

I never resorted to violence, but this young woman was tempting me. Her accusations and insults had gotten on the one last nerve I had left. I put my hand on Luella's shoulder and moved her gently to the side. Chloe flinched when I stepped closer to her. I shivered as the temperature fell and the cold set in. The courtyard was silent except for the fountain. The water rushed down in spurts now, splashing onto the surrounding tiles. Out of the corner of my eye, I noticed the jasmine flowers seemed bigger than before. I had a sense of strength I had only felt twice in my life: giving birth to Olivia and telling her father to get lost after I discovered his infidelities.

"I'm going to give you the benefit of the doubt. You're young and apparently weren't raised with any manners. I don't care if you're from a good family or the future of this supposed coven." I paused when the crowd gasped. "My focus is to figure out my options with this house."

Chloe opened her mouth, but closed it when I took a step backward. She pursed her lips, and she wrapped her arms around her body. But there was fear in her eyes, not the emotion I expected from her. I assumed she would be angry, not scared.

"Let me say this." I scanned the crowd, noting a mix of rage, indignation, and shock from the group. "This house isn't the only reason I'm here. Luella said my mother was murdered, and I want to know why someone would want her dead."

Water gushed out of the water fountain, the sound almost as loud as the women's protests. I noticed a few women nodding instead of shouting. Did they believe my mother was murdered, too?

I didn't have time to find out if anyone shared my opinion. Luella shushed the group and stood next to me. The water in the fountain came out as a trickle, and the air grew warm again. Everyone focused on Luella.

"Ladies, I am appalled at your behavior. I know some of you hold Fern responsible for those tragic deaths. She wasn't, and Althea isn't to be treated as a pariah." Luella put her hand on my arm. "Thea, I understand you're grieving for your momma and you know nothing about us. But I need you to give us a chance; give your abilities a chance to blossom. Only then will you realize we're your family, not the enemy."

The words that formed in my head were not positive, so I kept my mouth shut. I didn't expect to make friends with these women, especially if I sold the house. But Luella's calm, supportive words made me want to return it in kind. I nodded instead of speaking.

Chloe stomped over to a group of women her own age, standing by the fountain. She took a purple rhinestone-encrusted water bottle from her purse and took a drink.

"Ew, Chloe, your tea stinks! How can you drink that stuff?" asked a woman standing next to her.

"Because it makes me look fabulous. My skin glows, and I feel great." She put the bottle down on the edge of the water fountain and took a compact out of her purse. After tucking a piece of hair behind her ear, she snapped the compact shut and put it in her bag. "You should try it, Lauren. Your complexion could use the help. So could your stomach. How much weight have you gained this week?"

Lauren rested her hands on her stomach, which did not need any help. But then again, Chloe was rail thin and evidently, thought anyone of normal weight was fat. As Lauren rushed away, the other women stared at the ground. She went toward an opening, left of the main building.

"Chloe Chase, your momma would have slapped you upside your head if she were here." A woman around my age with long auburn hair held back with a green headband strode over to the younger witch. She wore jeans, a matching T-shirt, and a cardigan in flamingo pink.

"My momma can't be here because of her mother." Chloe jerked her head in my direction. "Why are you defending her, Evangeline?"

"Your momma isn't here because she fell in love with a talentless piano player in Key West." Evangeline snorted. "Candace would want us to treat Althea like she's one of us because she is. Fern didn't kill your grandmother, and your mother agrees with me."

"Excuse me, but what are you accusing my mother of doing?" I shook Luella's hand off my arm and walked close to Chloe and Evangeline.

"She condemned them to the afterlife for all eternity!" Chloe snarled.

Condemned two women to the afterlife? What in the world did that even mean? This woman, this entire group, was nuts.

"Chloe, it's time for you to go." Luella pointed toward the exit. "Actually, everyone should leave now, too. We'll reconvene tomorrow night once Thea has had time to settle in. I mean it. Get going!"

The women exited through the former carriageway which led to the sidewalk in front of the house. Some avoided eye contact with me, others smiled, and a couple glared. Chloe hadn't moved. "Althea Fontenot, you should just go now. You're not welcome here."

"Chloe Chase, you're the one who is leaving and the one who is not welcome in *my* home." I raised my voice so everyone could hear.

"Are you trying to banish me from the coven?" Chloe's voice rose at least two octaves. "You can't do that! Can she, Luella?"

"She's not banishing you. She didn't say that." Luella gulped. "Let's start over tomorrow. Evangeline, would you walk Chloe out, please?"

"I can leave on my own, but this isn't over." Chloe held her head up high and turned on her heels. If she had planned to make a dramatic exit, she ruined it by tripping over a slate tile. She caught herself before falling over and kept going without looking back at the courtyard. Thankfully she didn't; otherwise, she would have seen Tasso rolling on the ground and laughing.

"Tasso, behave yourself!" Luella snapped.

"Fine." Tasso stood up and came over to me. He rubbed against my jeans, leaving his orange fur all over my legs.

"Thea-Bea, you sure know how to make an entrance. I tell you what; that was the most fun I've had all year." Tasso trotted to the water fountain and jumped up on the ledge. With his paw, he knocked Chloe's water bottle into the fountain. "Someone needed to put that girl in her place, but now you've got an enemy. Not the smartest thing to do for a returning witch."

"You're right, Tasso, that fight won't make it easier for Thea to return to the fold," Evangeline said.

"Would you stop talking like I'm not here?" I walked over to the fountain to sit next to the cat. I studied him again, trying to figure out how someone was speaking as him.

"Honey, Tasso really is talking to you." Evangeline sat on the other side of the cat and scratched underneath his chin.

"You can read my mind, too?" I sighed. I had never considered ESP a real skill, but now I wondered.

"We can do all kinds of things. Once you remember, you'll be so excited. We had fun as kids making the jasmine grow." Evangeline pointed to the back wall. She flicked her wrist and said, "Let this flower bloom with speed faster than time. Its beauty to be shared with all, a moment so divine."

The vines sprouted, covering the entire wall and draping onto the ground. Jasmine flowers popped like popcorn in a machine. The buds grew, and their scent filled the air as if a bottle of perfume had shattered on the slate tiles. I was overcome with wonder and joy, like a child seeing snowflakes for the first time.

"Stop showing off, Evangeline. Put those back in their place or you're trimming them back." Luella's voice was sharp, but she smiled.

Evangeline flicked her wrist again and said, "Let this flower return to where it began. Its beauty will still be." As fast as the vines had grown, they shrunk to their original size. I rubbed my eyes, out of disbelief but also exhaustion. Today was all too much. After I ate and rested, I would demand Luella tell me how they did these tricks, and what Chloe meant by my mother condemning witches to the afterlife.

"I need to escape for a bit. Luella, do you have a key for

me?" I stood up, willing my legs not to wobble. I was light-headed because I hadn't eaten for hours. Who was I kidding? This entire experience of witches and magic drained my body and my mind. I just expected to see my house and sell it. Instead, I got lessons in magic and a confrontation with an insipid young woman.

And I couldn't forget that the coven thought my mother was a killer. What else was I going to learn?

5

———

Luella handed me a key and darted into the house. Tasso jumped onto the courtyard wall and disappeared over the side. Evangeline followed me into the house, and I grabbed my purse.

"I gather we were childhood friends, so you won't mind telling me who my mother supposedly murdered," I asked her once we were outside the house. Luella was nowhere to be found.

"Yes, we were friends, but Luella needs to tell you the story. I will say that a spell didn't go as planned. Your mother was the only survivor."

A talking cat, jasmine vines growing and shrinking at will, and now a magic spell gone wrong. Not the information I was expecting to get from this trip here.

"I'm sorry to upset you." Evangeline pulled me into a hug. I stiffened, not used to being hugged by strangers. As she held me, my body relaxed. I needed comforting, but I thought I'd find it in a pint of ice cream. My friend group had disappeared over the years as our connection through our children ended when our kids graduated. And having quit my job, my work friends were gone too. Evangeline's embrace made me hope she would be my friend. At least as long as I was here.

"Thank you. I just want to learn what happened with my mother," I said.

"Now, don't your worry. You're going to get your powers back, and everything will be right as rain. But I need to ask you to do something for me."

"Please tell me it doesn't involve spells or a talking cat. I've had enough magic for one day."

Laughter erupted from Evangeline's fuchsia lips. "Oh, honey, this is just the tip of the iceberg. You'll get used to it all soon enough. I promise."

While I doubted that, I just smiled. "What do you want me to do?"

"Put on your momma's necklace. I know it's in your purse. You should wear it all the time, but especially here in New Orleans."

"Why?"

"It identifies you as part of the Fontenot Coven. Your status as a witch will protect you, but the necklace offers extra security. Since you don't have all your powers yet, you need it even more."

"Protection from what? How is a necklace going to help if I'm mugged?" I opened my purse and took out my mother's necklace. I didn't want to hurt Evangeline's feelings, even though I doubted a necklace could be used as a weapon. "From Chloe? Or are there vampires and werewolves here too?"

"Vampires, witches, and werewolves, oh my!" Evangeline's laugh lit up her face. "Now, don't you worry about Chloe. We'll all keep an eye on her. But please wear the locket, even if it's just to humor an old friend."

I had to admit, I'd always wanted to try on my mother's necklace. She never gave me the chance, no matter how much I asked. My mother always wore it, including in the shower. In her will, she demanded I destroy the necklace, but I couldn't. It wasn't the first time, or the last time, that I would disobey my mother. The necklace felt comfortable, like I had worn it forever.

"It looks perfect. Now, I'm sorry I can't stay, but I've got a meeting with a client. I'll come by tomorrow morning, and we can go to breakfast. I hope you still like beignets." Evangeline rushed down the street but gave a quick wave before turning the corner.

I considered going back inside and demanding Luella tell me everything, but my grumbling stomach convinced me otherwise. I had to stay here for at least a week, so I'd have time to grill her for information. My mother wasn't a murderer. She couldn't even kill bugs that got in the house, so how would she have murdered two people? But now I understood at least one reason my mother left the city. Being accused of murder would be enough, or was there something else that drove her away?

But right now, I needed to find food. The thought of sitting down at a restaurant by myself wasn't appealing. I would make do with groceries from a convenience store to satisfy my hunger.

Ten blocks from Fontenot Mansion, I found a little corner store. Rows of groceries ended at a large deli counter. I stared at the list of sandwiches, overwhelmed by the variety.

Muffuletta? Po' boy?

The kind man behind the counter described a muffuletta as having Italian cold cuts, cheese, and olive salad. They make the sandwich on special sesame-seed-covered bread that is baked in a round shape.

A po' boy sandwich was like a sub sandwich, but on French bread. They can fill it with meat or seafood. He favored the fried shrimp po' boy, dressed. I took his recommendation after he told me dressed meant it had lettuce, tomato, mayonnaise, and pickles.

I picked up a six-pack of diet soda and two bottles of wine. After careful consideration, I added a pint of rocky road ice cream; the name was apropos for my situation.

The road continued to be rocky as I walked back to Fontenot Mansion. Seeing the houses up close made me lose track of time and my location. As the sky darkened and the gaslights grew brighter, I grew a bit concerned about being lost. I put my grocery bag down and took out my phone to study the map. My navigation skills were lacking, but I could set the map app to read out the directions as I walked. After putting in my address, I picked up my bag and started back to Fontenot Mansion.

Walking down the street, the first voice I heard wasn't from my phone, but from a stranger behind me.

"Hello, there. Need some help?"

"No, thanks. I'm good." Normally I would have looked over my shoulder and then kept on my way. Tonight I stopped after I saw the man behind me.

Wearing blue jeans, a white T-shirt, and a well-worn black leather jacket, he looked like a blond version of James Dean. He was six feet tall and muscular, but that didn't intimidate me. His green eyes staring at me did, though. The way he fiddled with a silver chain that hung from his right side jeans pocket worried me, too. Did he have a weapon on the end of it?

"Are you sure? The bag is heavy, and you look lost. I'm

happy to help a newcomer to our fair city." His voice was smooth, with just a slight hint of a Southern accent. His eyes studied me like an animal watching its prey. "By the way, that's a pretty necklace you've got there."

"I'm fine." I shifted my heavy grocery bag from one hand to the other. I'd heard about Southern hospitality, but I didn't believe that was the reason he stopped me. The lightness of his voice didn't match the darkness of his eyes. Having worked in the sketchy part of Seattle for years, I recognized that look of aggression lying beneath his polite manner.

"No, you're not fine. Let me help you." The man stepped toward me, and I dropped my grocery bag on his foot as I stumbled backward.

"I'm going to take my groceries and go." I reached for my bag, and as I bent over, my mother's necklace swung forward. As I clutched it in my hand, a sense of strength enveloped me. My mother's words whenever I came home from school after being bullied, reverberated in my mind: "Stand up for yourself, Thea! You are stronger than they are."

Facing a tall, intimidating man was not the same as being chased by a small boy. But that inner courage my mother ingrained in me exploded out of me in words.

"Listen, I said I am fine. Leave me alone." I lashed out and gripped my bag tighter. The sky darkened, and the air grew colder the longer I stood in front of this man. The chills down my spine made me shudder, and it became worse when he stepped closer. Any semblance of helpfulness disappeared as he grabbed my hand holding my necklace. I squeezed the locket tighter, but almost released it when it vibrated.

The man gritted his teeth as he tried to pry my hand off

my necklace. I willed my body to run, but my feet wouldn't move. A strange heat from the necklace ran up my arm and spread across my body. My heart pounded and my ears buzzed. My attacker released his hand as I wrenched myself from his grasp. I almost fell over my grocery bag, but caught my footing in time.

"Give me the necklace, or I'll make things worse for you." His hands once again reached for my necklace.

I couldn't concentrate on his hands; the fangs that glimmered in his mouth were more concerning.

6

———

Fangs. Yes, this man had fangs. They had to be those cheap plastic things. But they looked real. In horror movies, the victim stands there and screams her head off, or she runs. I refused to do either.

I picked up my grocery bag while keeping my eyes on the stranger. "You can't have my necklace. Leave me alone, or I'll call the police."

"Are you brave or stupid? I'm not sure yet." The man snorted and dropped his hands. "For once, my meal hasn't run away in a panic. What a shame, since I love fast food."

Meal? This guy was playing the vampire role too well. I needed to get out of here before he tried to bite my neck. I suspected I couldn't outrun the guy, and he would definitely grab my cell phone from me faster than I could dial 9-1-1. Screaming for help was moot since the street was empty. I had to depend on myself.

"We can do this the easy way or the hard way." The man stepped closer and tilted his head. The smile on his face as he ran his tongue over his teeth was all I needed to decide.

I grabbed the wine bottles from the bag and bashed

them together. The glass shattered, and the alcohol splashed my shoes and the sidewalk. I clutched the necks of each bottle and pointed them at the man.

"Go now or I'll cut you!" I yelled, hoping my terror didn't come through my voice. I focused on keeping my hands from shaking, but also thinking of what part of his body I should thrust my last-minute weapons into. Physically, I stood no chance against him, but I wouldn't go down without a fight.

"Death by bottles sounds like one of those silly mystery books my grandma used to read." The man laughed.

"Then go away, and no one will get hurt with these bottles." I willed my body to stand tall as I prayed someone would come and help me.

Luella answered my prayer.

"Althea, why did you waste two perfectly good bottles of wine on that fool of a vampire?" Luella suddenly appeared in between me and the man. She faced him, her arms crossed.

"My dear Miss Lulu, you know this woman?" He spoke to Luella, but he locked eyes with me.

"Yes, Trent. Althea just returned to the fold."

"Isn't she too old to learn new tricks?" Trent sneered.

"Isn't that the pot calling the kettle black? You're almost a hundred, but you still have training wheels on your wings." Luella stepped backward to stand side by side with me.

"You're such a witch." He stomped off and changed into a bat.

Yes, a bat. Flapping his wings, he flew straight into a streetlight, bounced off it and disappeared into the night.

Luella held her stomach as she laughed. "That boy has no manners and is the worst flyer of the colony."

"What happened? What kind of joke is this?" I gulped in the night air, hoping it would clear the confusion in my mind. Between witches, talking cats, and now vampires, I must have lost my mind.

"It's no joke. Trent actually is a young vampire since he's only been one for about seventy years, but I like to rile him up about his age when I can."

"You do it every time you see him, Miss Lulu," an unfamiliar voice said.

Out of nowhere, a cloud of fog appeared in front of us and a man walked out of it. The sudden fog wasn't as surprising as the man who arrived with it. His bespoke gray suit fit his six-foot two-inch body perfectly. He studied me with warm green eyes flecked with gold as he tightened his grip on the instrument case in his left hand. I returned his smile as he made me feel comfortable, even though his arrival was unusual. While he was formally dressed, and his glossy black hair was slicked back, he had an ease about him. It was as if he fit into any setting.

"You know I can't resist teasing him. But this time, you need to put Trent in his place, Atlas. He tried to attack one of my own," said Luella, also known as Lulu, I had learned.

"I'm sure he didn't realize this woman was with your coven." Atlas smiled at Luella and then at me. "I'm Atlas McCarthy. Who might you be?"

The hint of an Irish accent as he spoke surprised me in this Southern town. Between his good looks and charming accent, I just stared at him. Luella elbowed me.

"Oh, hi, I'm Althea."

I dropped the necks of the wine bottles to accept his handshake. I flinched at the coolness of his hand. "I'm sorry, I haven't had dinner yet, so my hand is freezing."

"What does dinner have to do with it?" I blurted. The

coolness didn't bother me any longer. There was a comfort to his touch, a softness to his skin.

Luella pulled me away from him. "I have got to teach you so much, child. He's cold because he has no blood. Atlas is a vampire."

7

"Althea, are you all right?" Atlas grasped my elbow when I stumbled backward.

His touch had been comforting before, but now it scared me. I jerked my arm from him and studied his face. He didn't have fangs like Trent, and he hadn't turned into a bat, so he couldn't be a vampire. What in the world was I thinking? Vampires don't exist.

"I'm fine. Is this how you treat tourists here? Do you set up cameras and fog machines? You must have bucketfuls of plastic fangs. All that's missing is a cape." I put my hands on my hips, hoping I appeared confident.

"Show her." Luella sighed.

Atlas smiled, showing off a set of fangs. As I stared at Atlas, I became light-headed and nauseous. Could he be a vampire?

"Yes, child, he is a vampire." Luella put her arm around me.

"You don't know about vampires? Didn't your mother tell you?" Atlas raised his eyebrows.

"You weren't here when Fern left, so you don't know Althea's history," Luella said. "She just returned today."

"You're Fern's daughter? I should have recognized the famous Fontenot hair." Atlas studied me intently, so much so that I wondered if I should run away. "How is Fern? I was sorry she left New Orleans before I returned."

"She died a few weeks ago." I clutched her necklace.

"She did? I just saw her at my club," he said.

"Atlas, dear, that was thirty years ago." Luella put her hand on his arm.

"Oh." Atlas looked down at the sidewalk. "I'm not very good at recognizing the passing of time, am I?" He raised his head and patted Luella's hand on his arm.

"Aren't we all?" Luella removed her hand from his arm.

"Althea, I am sorry for your loss, no matter when it occurred." Atlas pointed at the necklace. "You're wearing the coven's necklace. Hold on a minute."

Atlas moved his mouth, but I didn't hear any words. I turned to Luella. "What's he doing?"

"Just wait," she said.

Another cloud of fog developed next to Atlas, and Trent appeared in it. "You rang, Attie?"

"Yes." Atlas frowned. "Why did you approach Althea? She's wearing a coven necklace. We don't provoke them by our law and on principle."

"She's wearing a necklace?" Trent stepped toward me but stopped when Atlas put his hand on his shoulder. "I didn't see it."

What a liar!

Luella said, *Say nothing. We'll deal with him later.*

I turned to her, my mouth gaping open. Her words didn't shock me; it was the fact I heard her words in my head. Great, not only did she read my mind, but she could get into it. Would she dig around in it? I didn't want her, or anyone, for that matter, prying into my private thoughts.

"This is Althea, a member of the Fontenot Coven. You may apologize to her now, Trent," Atlas said.

"Sorry, Althea. It won't happen again." Trent bowed toward me and Luella. "Happy now? You're late for your set, Attie-boy. Shouldn't you go?"

"Don't call me Attie-boy." Atlas dropped his arm off Trent's shoulder after giving it a squeeze. Trent winced, and I bit the inside of my lip so I wouldn't smile at his pain.

"Fine, let's go, *Atlas*." Trent didn't turn into a bat, but walked down the street.

"Again, my apologies, Althea and Miss Lulu." Atlas smiled. This time, his fangs weren't showing. "Welcome back to New Orleans, Thea."

With that, Atlas followed Trent down the street. I stared after him until he disappeared around the corner.

"Don't get any romantic ideas about Atlas—"

"Not a problem," I interrupted Luella. "I'm not interested in him."

"I don't need magic to see you two are attracted to each other."

"You need eyeglasses, then. We were just being polite, nothing more," I lied. Yes, Atlas caught my eye, but he was a vampire. A supposed vampire. I had encountered some strange men on dating apps, but never a vampire.

"Keep it that way. You can't get involved with a one."

"Luella, I'm not here for a vacation romance." My romantic life had been lacking for the past few years, but I wasn't desperate enough to date a man who claimed to be a vampire. Even though he had bright eyes, a strong jawline, and thick dark hair, all the features I found attractive in men.

"This isn't a vacation, child. You have a lot to learn." She shook her head. "But for now, let's get back home. There's a cold bottle of wine in the refrigerator, and we'll clean those tennis shoes."

I looked down at my wine-splattered shoes and the shards of glass surrounding my feet. "I don't have much hope to save those shoes. Shouldn't we pick up the glass?"

Luella said, "Remove these broken wares as I decree. Cleanse this place and make it as it should be."

The broken wine bottles disappeared. I rubbed my eyes in disbelief. My sticky hands stung my eyes, and the floral notes of the wine overwhelmed my nose.

"I don't know how you keep doing all this around here. You need to explain it to me." I picked up my grocery bag.

"Let's go home. The street isn't any place to talk about our business." Luella took my bag from me and, with her other hand, steered me toward Fontenot Mansion.

"Fine, but you won't get out of talking to me. I want answers."

"You'll get your answers. I promise."

After what I'd seen in the few hours I'd been in New Orleans, I could use a glass of wine, or three. As long as my drink came with the truth about what was really going on here.

8

———————

The thought of wine and answers kept me going even though my feet were begging me to stop. I'd walked more today than I had all of last week. I'd need to buy a new pair of tennis shoes for tomorrow.

There were cars parked along the streets, but I didn't see any garages. Of course, they built most of the homes when horse-drawn carriages were the mode of transportation. We reached Fontenot Mansion, and a wave of sadness hit me. Logically, I understood it wasn't unheard of that I didn't have memories of my life here. I wished I remembered growing up in this mansion, surrounded by a tight-knit group of people. My life in Seattle was the complete opposite of what Luella claimed my childhood was here. Then again, normal people would want to forget about growing up in a coven.

I opened the gate with the key. It was a struggle to make it turn, as if it hadn't been used for years.

"You won't need that key soon," Luella said.

"Because I'll be gone from here?"

"No, because any witch in our coven can automatically

open the gate. We don't need keys for our meeting place. Once I figure out how to get your powers back, you won't need it."

"So I'll be able to make jasmine grow, read minds, and open gates without keys." I rolled my eyes. "But I can't date vampires."

"Yes, yes, yes, and yes to all that, Miss Smarty-Pants." Luella brushed past me and stomped up the stairs. "I wish you would take this seriously, Althea."

"Yes, ma'am," I whispered. Luella whipped her head around, her lips pursed as if she was going to yell at me. She didn't, so I assumed she heard the sincerity in my voice. While I still didn't accept her magic claims, she stopped a potential mugger from robbing me. I should treat her with more respect, but I was still irritated that she hadn't told me the entire story about my mother yet.

"I see your Southern manners are coming back to you." I held the front door open for Luella as she gave me a slight smile. "You've had a rough day and I should think of how strange this must be to you."

"Strange is an understatement." I followed Luella through the hallway to the kitchen. Every few feet, an icy breeze would pass by me. "Luella, or Miss Lulu, the house seems to have several drafts. Are there are a lot of repairs that need to be done?"

"You haven't told her yet, have you?" Tasso sat on top of the worn wood table in the center of the room. Luella placed the grocery bag right next to Tasso and picked him up. "Hey, put me down!"

"Then don't keep getting up on the table like I told you." Luella plopped Tasso onto the floor, where he cleaned his face.

"Great, more bad news for me." I opened the refrigerator

and pulled out a bottle of wine. "I should have expected the house needed repairs."

Tasso stopped licking his face. "The house needs work, but I tell you what, it's not that kind of work."

"What do you mean by that?" I began opening drawers, looking for a bottle opener.

"He means nothing." Luella opened a drawer next to her and pulled out a bottle opener. She let it slip as she handed it to me. "Something is wrong, terribly wrong."

"I'd say so. That bottle of wine is horrible. You should have bought moonshine from Amos down in the bayou." Tasso had jumped back onto the table and sniffed the bottle.

"Hush, Tasso!" Luella grasped her necklace. I did the same, surprised that the locket was cool in my hand. I squeezed my eyes shut, and an image of the water fountain in the courtyard flashed before my eyes. The water gushed from the top, splashing into the bottom tier. A rhinestone water bottle bobbed in the clear blue water before it bumped into a head hanging over the edge of the fountain. I opened my eyes to see Luella's expression of fear. Had she seen what I had seen?

I didn't stop to ask her. Luella followed me as I rushed out the backdoor. Just as I had seen in my mind, the waterfall was running, and the person I saw was hanging over the edge.

Chloe's head was under the water.

9

―――――

I grabbed Chloe's shoulder and flipped her over. Her glazed eyes and slack jaw told me all I needed to know —she was dead. I gulped down the bile that tried to escape. In the few minutes I'd spent with Chloe, I didn't like her, but I wouldn't have wished her dead. I imagined how devastated I'd be to find my daughter like this.

"Luella, do something! If you're the witch you say you are, make her come back to life!" I snapped.

"I can't bring her back to life, Thea. It's not allowed," Luella murmured.

"Wait a minute, you can bring her back to life, but you won't?" I sat down on the edge of the fountain.

"Now you believe I'm a witch? Here we are with a dead woman and now you trust me! Althea Fontenot you will be the death of me yet." Luella shook her finger at me.

"Poor choice of words, don't ya think?" Tasso appeared next to me, his paws on my lap.

I scratched the top of his head, something I had done with all my cats. I expected him to yell at me, because surely a talking cat didn't want to be treated as a regular one. But he let me pet him and even purred.

"I don't know what I believe anymore. But for now, that doesn't matter. We need to call the police," I said.

"Yes, we do, but I must do this first." Luella stood over Chloe's body. "Rest, dear soul, as your time has passed. Seek your ancestors as they will guide you steadfast."

I waited awkwardly, not sure if I should say or do something. I whispered, "Amen" in the hope that was enough for me to do.

"Amen indeed." Luella pulled out her cell phone and went to the back of the courtyard.

"Tasso, are you actually a talking cat?" I couldn't believe I was asking an animal this question, but with Luella occupied, she couldn't do a ventriloquist act. And anything was better than thinking about Chloe in the fountain.

"Well, I ain't a talking dog. Of course I'm a cat." Tasso squinted at me. "Now hold on cher; you believe in magic now?"

"Why are you calling me sha?"

Tasso meowed five times in a row, which I took as a laugh. "You say sha, but it's spelled c-h-e-r. It's a Cajun way of saying dear. I can be nice."

"Thanks." I stared at him, trying to figure out if this was really a magical experience. "I guess you could say I'm becoming more open-minded about magic."

"Good on ya! You'll get there." Tasso jumped down and started toward the back of the courtyard. "Now I'm going to get. The police will shoo me out of here."

"Before you go, did you see Chloe come back to the courtyard?" I asked.

Tasso swished his tail and kept walking. I guess I

shouldn't have expected an answer from a cat, even a magic cat.

I clasped my necklace again, finding it cool and sturdy in my hand. It offered a sense of comfort I hadn't expected. My mother would have laughed at my sentimentality. She wasn't much for it, but I'm glad I had an emotional connection to objects. Especially since I believed this was more than a locket. Luella showed up when I held the locket as Trent the vampire tried to attack me. And then there was the vision of Chloe when I squeezed the locket. And I was sure Trent wanted the necklace.

As I heard the wail of sirens just outside the courtyard gate, I wished the locket could turn back time. The death of a young woman might have been prevented. Or at least, I wouldn't be in the middle of it. I shivered, but it wasn't from the cool breeze that brushed by me. I could no longer ignore the dead woman in my backyard, and everything a police investigation would bring.

10

The sirens stopped, and Luella let the police in through the courtyard gate. I took a seat at a table near the fountain, but avoided looking at Chloe's body. Luella sat across from me without a word.

Two uniformed officers headed straight to Chloe's body, but the man following them came right to Luella and me.

"Knox, I'm glad you're here." Luella stood up and accepted a kiss on her cheek from the man.

They made an odd pair, with the man towering over Luella. She was petite, but the man was at least six feet four inches. A brown tweed suit barely contained his bulging muscles. Thick, wavy brown hair skimmed the collar of his white button-down shirt.

"It was the luck of the draw I was assigned the case. Unless you put a spell on my captain, Miss Lulu."

"My lips are sealed." Luella motioned as if she had zipped her lips shut. "But honestly, I am thankful you're here. I'm afraid Chloe's death is most likely because of magic."

I waited for Knox to laugh or ask what in the world

Luella was talking about. He did neither. In fact, he appeared to believe her as he nodded his head.

"Knox, let me introduce you to Althea. She returned to New Orleans today," Luella said.

I stood up and accepted Knox's firm handshake. "Hello. You must be a detective with the New Orleans Police."

"Yes, ma'am. Name is Knox Dupriest. I'm with the homicide division." Knox turned to look at the fountain. "There's no chance this was an accident, is there?"

"I doubt it. I didn't see any abrasions on her head or defensive wounds on her hands. And her face has a yellow undertone, which she didn't have earlier," I said.

Both Luella and Knox stared at me, making me squirm. "Miss Althea, Luella said you returned to New Orleans. What's your business here?"

"She's a Fontenot, Knox!" Luella said.

"Oh, you're a witch, not a detective, then?" Knox said.

"I'm neither, but yes, my name is Fontenot. So you believe in witchcraft?" I rubbed my temples, wishing my newly formed headache would disappear.

"Of course he does! Knox is a..." Luella started, but Knox put his hand up as if he were stopping traffic.

"Let's just say here in New Orleans, we believe in many things, and many of them contradict each other." Knox took out a tan leather notebook and fountain pen. This man had elegant and expensive taste. "But there's no gray area when it comes to murder. So, Miss Fontenot, tell me, did you kill Chloe Chase?"

"I did not!" I spat every word out, even though my mouth was as dry as a desert. "Listen, Detective Dupriest, I just arrived today and only met Chloe a few hours ago. While we didn't hit it off, I had no reason to want her dead."

"It was just a question, Miss Fontenot." Knox's amber

eyes seemed to glow yellow for a moment. I needed sleep; now I was seeing strange things in everyone I met in this town.

"Let's get on with finding out who really killed Chloe." Luella stabbed her finger on Knox's notebook. "You need to get actual information to write down in that fancy book of yours."

"Yes, ma'am." Knox walked toward the fountain with Luella nipping at his heels. The thought of looking at Chloe's body again made my stomach churn, but I had to go over there. As the new owner of this house, I needed to be involved in any incidents on the property. I couldn't let a police investigation keep me from moving forward with my plans to sell the home. But I put that concern away for the time being as I imagined Chloe's family learning of her death.

Knox instructed the police officers to block off the entry to the house and to direct the coroner back here as soon as she arrived.

"Althea, you're right. Chloe looks yellow," Luella said as the three of us studied Chloe's face.

"Ms. Fontenot, could you tell me how you found Ms. Chase?" Knox said.

I skipped the part of how I saw the image of Chloe's body while I stood in the kitchen, clasping my necklace. "When I came out here, Chloe was draped over the bottom tier of the fountain. I turned her over and saw right away that she was dead."

"How were you sure?" Knox asked.

"Her face was frozen and her pupils were dilated." I shuddered. "She wasn't breathing."

"Did you think to do CPR?" Knox said.

"Just look at Chloe, Knox! We knew she was gone."

Luella lowered her voice. "There was nothing we could do with CPR or magic to bring her back."

Knox tilted his head to the side. "I've heard otherwise, but that's neither here nor there. Is that her purse?"

Luella pointed to Chloe's designer handbag next to her body. "Yes. It was closed when we got here."

"Her bottle is in the fountain." I pointed to the purple rhinestone-encrusted bottle bobbing in the water. "Maybe she came back for it."

"She carried her bottle all the time, drinking her own tea blend," Luella said.

"Chloe's necklace is gone," I said.

"No, it can't be." Luella fanned herself with her hand and went to sit on the edge of the fountain. Knox gently grasped Luella's elbow before she did.

"I'm sorry, Miss Lulu, but you can't sit there. Let's go back to the table." Knox led Luella away and I followed. My heart broke for her family, and going by the strain on Luella's face, this would be difficult for their group.

And for me, too. While it felt wrong to think of myself when Chloe was dead, I couldn't help it. I argued with her about selling the house just hours before her murder. Not only would this murder delay my plans, but from Knox's questions, I worried he considered me a viable suspect. I wasn't a killer, but would anyone believe me?

11

It was a long day, and it just got longer. Knox asked more questions and then sent Luella and me inside the house. Luella dropped into one of the kitchen chairs. Her pained expression didn't change as I rooted around in the cupboards for glasses. I took two crystal wine glasses out and poured each of us a generous amount of the now lukewarm wine. It didn't bother us, but I put it back into the refrigerator as we drank in silence.

"I haven't used these glasses for over forty years. It's a shame because they are so lovely." Luella raised her glass in the air. The kitchen lights illuminated the etched images of suns and moons on the glass.

I bit my lip so I wouldn't snap at Luella. Wine glasses weren't important right now. But when I noticed the tears meandering down her tense face, I gave her a moment of peace. After she wiped her tears, I said, "I can see you're upset about Chloe's death, but you were also worried about Chloe's missing necklace. Is there something significant about it?"

"You're gonna learn about this at some point anyway, so I

might as well tell you now." Luella gulped half of her wine. "Here you go. Much of our power comes from our necklace. Wearing it alerts other witches that we're from the Fontenot Coven. We use the locket for certain spells and rituals and we also use it to communicate with each other in times of trouble. That's how I found you with the vampire."

Now it was my turn to gulp half of my wine. A magical necklace for performing spells and calling for help. Is the locket like a Life Alert button? "My witch powers are blocked, so how could I have used it?"

"You are as sassy as your momma." Luella frowned, but a slight smile crept on her face. "Fern apparently didn't suppress all your powers. I'm glad to see your mother had the sense to give you the ability to reach out for help."

"So you're saying the necklace told you I was in trouble? Why didn't you or anyone else come to Chloe's aid?"

Luella shook her head and pushed her chair back. With a shaking hand, she opened the refrigerator and took the wine back out. I doubted it was my question that caused her anxiety; she must have thought the same thing about Chloe.

"Either she didn't have time to use her necklace or she didn't think the person she was with would harm her. Or she was poisoned earlier," I said. "Do you know anyone who would want to kill her?"

I took the wine bottle from Luella's hand and refilled our glasses. She clutched her glass so hard, I was afraid it would shatter in her hand. I took it from her and placed it on the table. "Luella, I don't mean to upset you, but Chloe's death most likely wasn't random. Most murders aren't."

"I agree. This wasn't random. Your mom was the third witch to be killed this month, and now Chloe's the fourth." Luella picked up her glass and took a sip. "And I'm afraid she won't be the last."

This time, the wineglass shook in my hand, and it was Luella who took the glass from me. I slumped against the back of my chair with my arms hanging limply at my sides.

"I'm sorry, Althea. I know you don't want to hear this, but someone has been killing witches from our coven. Betty fell down her stairs, broke her leg, and died in surgery. Donna died of carbon monoxide poisoning in her brand new house. Your mother was killed in a hit-and-run, and now Chloe is dead."

"Those all sound like accidents, except Chloe, of course."

"I don't think so. Betty was in perfect health, and the doctors couldn't figure out why she died. The batteries were brand new in the carbon monoxide detectors in Donna's home. And your mom was standing in broad daylight when that car hit her. These were murders!" Luella slapped her hand on the table, making the wine slop over the side of her glass.

"Okay, say the other witches were murdered. The big difference between the deaths is Chloe was poisoned and had her locket stolen. That didn't happen with the other witches. I have my mom's necklace," I said.

"I haven't told anyone else this, but Donna's necklace is missing." Her lips trembled. "Betty's daughter was there when her mother passed away so she took her necklace. But when I went to Donna's house after her neighbor called me, it was gone."

"Hmm." That didn't sound good, but it could just be a coincidence. But another thought came to mind. "Luella, do the necklaces get passed down from mother to daughter?"

"No, each witch gets her own with their family surname engraved on the back. You're the exception since your necklace went missing when you were a child."

"No one was concerned about that?"

"Your mother didn't notice it was gone until you were leaving the city. We just assumed we'd find it in the house or with your belongings in Seattle."

"If it was there, I didn't know about it." I frowned.

"Fern and I both did spells to find it, but had no luck. If you get your memories back, maybe you'll tell us where it is."

I rubbed my temples, praying it would make my headache go away. This day couldn't get any worse.

Oh, but it did.

"For the sake of argument, why would someone want to kill these women? And why take the necklaces?" I asked.

"They are trying to destroy our coven. Our powers are unusual. No other group of witches can do what we can do—"

"And what is it you do?" I interrupted.

"We are the witches who guard the living and the dead here in New Orleans."

12

Thankfully, I didn't have a mouthful of wine because I would have spit it at Luella. Guardians of the living and the dead? Don't witches cast spells over a bubbling cauldron?

"No, we do not use bubbling cauldrons, Althea Rose."

"Sorry, I forgot you could read my mind." Did I say that? It must be the wine talking.

"The sooner you believe what I tell you, the easier it will be for you." Luella sighed.

"Fine. What does it mean to guard the living and the dead?"

"The living and dead should exist in different worlds. People disturb the dead in the afterlife because of their interest in the paranormal."

"What's wrong with that?" I asked.

"If it's for a fleeting moment, it is fine, but more times than not, the living calls to the dead. Some try to bring them back. It upsets the balance of nature."

"Does this happen everywhere, or only in New Orleans?"

"New Orleans is unique in many ways, but our respect for the dead is more heartfelt here. Many of us here can connect with the dead, but not everyone does it for good." Luella frowned.

"It sounds like you spend more time protecting the dead from the living," I said.

"I'd say it's fifty-fifty."

Glass shattered in the other room. I jumped to my feet. "What was that?"

Was the killer here in the house? We didn't check or even ask the police to do it. I looked toward the knife block next to the oven, wondering if I should grab a knife or grab Luella and run outside.

Luella got up from her seat. "I'll go see. And don't worry, no one else is here in the house. I checked."

"When did you do that? We came inside together. Oh, you mean you did it with magic?"

"Now you're getting how things work in this house." Luella patted my arm as she passed me. "Sit back down, and I'll go clean up whatever mess Tasso made."

I did as she asked, and I grabbed the bag of chips I bought at the deli owner's suggestion. The Voodoo potato chips tasted like regular barbecue chips to me, so I don't know why they were named that way. Must be a marketing ploy for the tourists like the alligator sausage. Or was it actually made from alligator? Who eats alligator? The person to ask came through a cat door built into the backdoor.

"Thea-Bea, the police are still here and disrupting my evening." Tasso jumped onto the table and sniffed my chips. "The dill-pickle-flavored-chips are better."

"I'll make a note. Hey, do people actually eat alligator or is it chicken?"

Tasso narrowed his eyes. "Of course it's gator! Chicken is

chicken and gator is gator. You really have forgotten your Southern roots. Fried alligator on a stick was your favorite."

"Thea, it was just Tasso knocking things around..." Luella stopped talking when she entered the room.

"You blaming me again for messing up that ugly bric-a-brac in the living room?" Tasso jumped off the floor. "I'll go take care of them."

"Them?" I asked, but Tasso trotted out the door without answering. "Would you care to explain why you blamed Tasso for something he didn't do? And who is them?"

"Never mind that cat or me. I'm as tired as an ant at a church picnic." Luella pulled out a chair and plopped down.

I studied Luella's face. There were bags under her eyes, and her hair was loose around her face. Her shoulders were slumped as if they were holding the weight of the world. "Are you sure it was Tasso and not an intruder?"

"Yes, child. Tasso never accepts responsibility for his accidents." Luella closed her eyes.

I thought of arguing that Tasso couldn't have been the one making noise at the front of the house because he entered from the back. But I didn't, in case she was going to tell me that Tasso could teleport. I didn't think I could handle any more weirdness.

"Let's get back to this whole being-responsible-for-the-living-and-the-dead-thing you say your coven does."

Luella opened her eyes and sighed. "Let me put it in plain English for you. The living and the dead are not supposed to mingle. Neither one should try to bring the other into their world. The balance of nature must be respected and we do that by keeping them in their places."

"Okaaay..." I didn't bother to keep my disbelief out of my voice.

"Yes, it sounds strange, but we have seen the effects of this and it's not pretty."

"You mean hauntings?"

"I do. Many times, the dead won't leave and move on to the afterlife. Some are quiet, just observing the living, but many are disruptive, even deadly."

"Let me see if I understand." I drummed my fingers on the table. "Ghosts are real, but they're supposed to be in the afterlife. The living aren't supposed to bother the spirits. This means your coven is the referee between the living and the dead."

Luella laughed. "No one has put it that way, but I guess you can call us referees."

"And how do you do that?" I folded my arms.

"That's for another time, my dear. Once you have your powers back, you'll understand."

"Really? You're not going to tell me what I supposedly will be able to do? What do I need to do to gain these powers?"

"We'll do a ceremony, and before you ask, it doesn't include cauldrons."

"And I was looking forward to the cauldrons." I smiled, but then I remembered our earlier conversation. "Luella, can you at least tell me who would want to kill my mom and your other friends?"

"That's what we need to find out. It could be several other groups like the vampires, werewolves, the Voodoo community, or even other witches." Luella sighed. "Whoever it is, we need to stop them. If they keep killing our members, our coven will die, and with it, the balance between the living and the dead will disappear. Chaos will ensue."

13

———

I poured the last of the wine into my glass and downed it like a shot. I'd had enough of witchcraft for tonight. We sat in silence until Knox came inside.

"Luella, could you come outside with me for a minute? I need you to check the courtyard for anything that is missing."

"Did you find out how the person got into the court-yard?" I asked.

"There's no sign of forced entry," Knox said. "Who has keys to the house?"

"The coven can enter the house and the courtyard without keys. I just gave one to Thea tonight, but that's all. One of us is always here to let workers inside the house," Luella said.

"Could someone climb over the walls?" I said.

"Not unless they broke the spell," Luella said.

Once again, Knox didn't react to Luella's statement. Did everyone take magic seriously in this town?

"Okay, well, let's go outside. Ms. Fontenot, you aren't leaving town soon, are you?" Knox's expression hardened.

"We'll need you to come down to the station for an official statement."

"Now, Knox, Thea has nothing to do with Chloe's death. But she isn't leaving," Luella insisted.

"I'm here for the next week, but I'll check with you before I leave town," I said. "Now, I'd like to get some rest. It's been a long day, to say the least."

Knox gave me his card. "Call me tomorrow morning and we'll arrange a time to talk. I'm sorry we met under these circumstances, Ms. Fontenot."

"Your room is on the second floor, the first door on the left, in case you don't remember." Luella took the hand that Knox offered to her. He gently helped her up. "Fresh towels are in the bathroom. If you need me, I'm the last door on the right."

"You live here?" I said.

"Someone had to take care of this place." The indignation in Luella's voice was crystal clear. "Your mother's yearly visits weren't enough to keep this place running."

"Of course." I was too exhausted to defend my mother, or to ask if that was the real reason Luella wanted me to keep this house. I couldn't imagine living in this big place by myself, though.

After Luella and Knox left the kitchen, I washed our wine glasses and put them away. I took my suitcase from the living room where I had left it so many hours ago. The stairs creaked as I pulled my suitcase behind me. Cold air blew over me as I ascended, but once again, I didn't see an air vent anywhere. I would need to sell the house as-is since I had no desire to do any work on it.

I knew this was my room without Luella saying it. The door opened to walls painted in my favorite color: lilac. I closed the door behind me and put my suitcase down on the deep-purple, braided rug in front of the fourposter bed. All the furniture was a white shabby-chic style.

I went to the bookshelves to find it filled with my favorite childhood books. This collection mirrored my own back in Washington, from baby books to Nancy Drew novels. I opened *The Secret of the Old Clock* and my name, written in a child's handwriting, was there. Why didn't my mother take these books with us when we moved? Did we leave town so quickly that she couldn't pack them?

I shivered, from the cold, but also from melancholy. This colorful room was perfect for the book-and-purple-obsessed child I had been. Before I opened the closet door to look for an extra blanket, I noticed pencil marks along the frame. My mother noted my height from ages one to six on the door-frame. On the other side was my mother's name from ages one to eighteen. My height wasn't marked in our house in Seattle, but I did the same for my daughter.

I grabbed a purple blanket from the closet and wrapped it around my shoulders. My suitcases stood in the corner, waiting to be unpacked, but they would have to wait. I flopped on the bed and stared at the ceiling. I was still in a daze from the most bizarre day I'd ever had. I didn't know what to believe any more.

I did agree with Luella on one thing; my mother's death wasn't an accident. She was standing by her mailbox wearing her red parka. The sun was shining, so I wondered how the driver didn't see her. When I pointed out the tread marks in the road, the police said it could have been someone swerving to miss an animal running across the road, but hit my mother instead. Why would my mom be included in the supposed murder plot if she wasn't part of the coven?

My eyes fluttered as I sank deeper into soft down

pillows. My goal was to sell the house and move forward. Instead, I met a talking cat, a coven of witches, and two vampires. And then I found a dead woman in the courtyard of my family home. I gave in to my exhaustion, letting my eyes stay closed and pulling the blanket tighter around my body. A chill ran over me as I shifted, reminding me of the state of the house. I hoped that would be the only issue I faced on my second day in the French Quarter.

14

I slept in my clothes on top of the covers, but woke up at 7:00 a.m., feeling calm—until I remembered where I was and why I was here. I grabbed a set of clothes and my toiletry bag and headed toward the bathroom. The floorboards creaked as I walked down the hallway. Just like the living room, the walls were bare with traces of old art or photographs.

Fontenot Mansion's best insulated room was the bathroom. Even before I turned the hot tap on the clawfoot tub, the room was warm and cozy. If my bedroom was chilly again tonight, I might sleep here.

I glanced in the mirror one last time. Make-up saved me from a zombielike appearance. I covered up the circles under my eyes and a dash of a rosy shade of blush made me appear more rested than I felt.

At least my hair was on point. My mother, my daughter, and I all had thick blonde hair and wore it loose or pulled back in a ponytail. Atlas mentioned the Fontenot hair. And he smiled.

I had to put that handsome man out of my mind. Atlas

was attractive, but then again, he was as strange as everyone else in this town I'd met so far. Did he actually believe he was a vampire?

I pondered that as I walked down to the kitchen, but I cleared my mind before I entered the room. I didn't want Luella using her ESP on me. There must be an explanation for this skill. I hadn't found one yet, though.

"Do I smell cinnamon rolls?" I entered the kitchen to the aroma of fresh baked pastries.

"These are my world-famous orange cinnamon rolls." Evangeline took a tray out of the oven and placed it on top of the stove. "You can help me ice them."

"It's about time you woke up. I was about to send Tasso up to get you." Luella joined Evangeline at the stove. "Although now I've got to share these delicious rolls. You are such a wonderful baker, Evangeline."

"Excuse me, but it's not even eight o'clock yet. In fact, it's just six a.m. to me." I sat down at the table and picked up the newspaper. An article about Chloe's death was below the fold, which I imagined would have bothered her. While she wasn't top news, the photo they published was from her high school yearbook, and she looked lovely in her cap and gown. I was surprised the paper didn't publish a more recent photo.

"Where you graduated high school is more important than college. That's why they used that picture." Luella looked over my shoulder. "I remember Chloe's graduation from high school and college. Her momma threw parties for both that rivaled a Mardi Gras ball. Candace loved that girl more than anything, and she's hurting mighty bad today."

"I can only imagine. If I lost my daughter, I don't know what I'd do," I said.

"Candace will pull through as she always has." Luella

patted my shoulder. "She's lost many people in her life, but never from murder. This just adds another level of unimaginable pain."

Luella took a teacup and saucer from a cabinet. She placed it in front of me. "What kind of tea do you drink in the morning?"

"I don't drink tea. Do you have any coffee?"

Evangeline and Luella gasped, and if they were wearing pearls, they would have clutched them.

"Don't tell me witches can't drink coffee. That's a deal-breaker for me," I said.

"Sorry, you can't get out of being a witch because you like coffee." Evangeline grinned as she opened a cabinet next to the refrigerator. She pulled out a bag of coffee and a French press. "You're not the only witch who likes coffee."

"Why is tea so important to witches? Do you have to drink it to ride your brooms?" I said.

Evangeline cackled until Luella said, "Hush now. Stop being such a smarty-pants. Tea isn't a requirement, but we all drink it as it keeps us connected to nature."

Luella's stern face kept me from making a snarky retort. Instead, I asked, "Can you explain that? How are you connected to nature by tea?"

"Tea is a plant. Yes, I know coffee beans come from a plant." Luella put up her hand as if she expected I would interrupt her. "But tea has been a part of our culture more than coffee. And we read tea leaves, of course."

"Oh, of course." I rolled my eyes. "What do you mean you read leaves? I have no idea what you're talking about."

"We can read a person's future with tea leaves," Luella said.

"Before you ask, you can do it with coffee grounds. It's not our specialty, but perhaps it's something you can introduce to the coven." Evangeline's tone matched the smile on her face.

I wish I had an ounce of her positive nature this morning, but there was no chance I would without at least one cup of coffee. Fake it until you make it would have to be my mantra this morning. I forced a smile, which I hoped would lighten the mood.

"I should have known you drank coffee since you live in the land of the sirens." Luella snatched the tea cup and replaced it with a plain white coffee mug.

"What do you mean, the land of the sirens? Seattle has a ton of coffee companies—"

"Haven't you noticed that coffee company that has the mermaid logo? It's actually a siren. Knowing those sneaky fish, I bet they enticed the company to make them the figurehead. They've always been uppity," Luella said.

"Now, now, Luella, don't let Thea get the wrong impression about sirens. Some can be quite nice, but I'd be mad if I had two fins instead of legs," Evangeline said.

It was too early to talk about paranormal creatures.

Evangeline placed a creamer and sugar set by my mug, along with a silver spoon. "Thanks for the coffee, Evangeline."

"You're welcome, honey. Don't let Luella give you a hard time about drinking coffee. But you do like sweet tea, don't you?" Evangeline said.

"Sorry, I don't." I poured a dollop of cream and a spoonful of sugar into my mug. The first sip hit the spot with its warmth and deep roasted flavor. "What type of coffee is this? It's great."

"It's chicory coffee. I'm guessing the sirens don't use it." Evangeline laughed.

"When I'm back home, I'll ask the sirens to add it to the menu," I said.

"Oh, Althea dear, *this* is your home." Evangeline grasped my hand. "Once we restore your powers, this will feel like your home once again."

I sipped my coffee so I wouldn't make a snide comment. This wouldn't be my home, and there were no powers to restore. The only thing that had gone well so far was this new-to-me chicory coffee.

"Althea just needs time to adjust back." Evangeline took a long drink. "Hmm, I make a fine cup of coffee."

"I still say tea is better. Do you want me to ice these cinnamon rolls?" Luella said.

"I won't say no to your help." Evangeline joined Luella at the counter. As they worked on the cinnamon rolls, they whispered under their breath.

I closed my eyes and savored the drink. At least they had excellent coffee here and, by the smell of it, yummy pastries. Just as I relaxed, the thud on the table ruined it.

"Thea-Bea, look at you all grown-up and drinking coffee."

I opened my eyes to find Tasso staring at me. "Do magical cats drink coffee?"

"Only when Miss Evangeline makes it. Luella just drinks that weak tea," he said.

"So you don't like tea either. We have one thing in common," I said.

"I tell you what, if you learn to make coffee like Miss E., I promise to give you all the gossip around here. You wouldn't believe what witches are up to these days." Tasso dipped his paw into the creamer and licked his paw.

"How many times have I told you to ask for cream

instead of helping yourself?" Luella lifted Tasso and placed him on the floor.

"You take all the fun out of it." Tasso meowed and trotted over to Evangeline, who placed a saucer of cream at his feet. "Whatcha all doing this morning?"

"We're going to restore Althea's powers," Luella answered.

"You don't say? This is your last chance to run, Thea. Once they do their mumbo jumbo, you're back to being a witch," Tasso said.

Evangeline and Luella gave Tasso the same dirty look, but neither said anything. Tasso was right. I could refuse or even leave. Well, I could refuse, but I couldn't leave, according to the detective.

But I wouldn't deny my curiosity about the ritual. Despite wanting to write it off as hogwash, the tingling on the back of my neck caused doubt. If I didn't go through with it, I'd never know what they believed I could do. But there was a feeling of dread that what I learned would change my life—and not necessarily for the better.

15

Even though the cinnamon rolls smelled amazing, the churning of my stomach prevented me from eating one. I promised Evangeline I'd try one after the ritual. Assuming I hadn't run off in fear or in laughter.

"We're going to the room where we keep the materials we need to perform rituals and the coven's special heirlooms," Luella said as she walked me down to the ground floor. The staircase led to the former carriageway. If we had turned right, we would have gone toward the courtyard. Instead, we turned left and entered the first door.

I gasped as I followed Luella into the room. In the center was a large, round table covered with a light-blue linen tablecloth. Jasmine vines were embroidered around all the edges of the cloth and real jasmine flowers floated in a silver bowl the size of a punchbowl. A candelabra with three different colored candles—white, brown, and purple—sat next to it. A shoebox-sized wooden box was the last item on the table.

To my left, a tall workbench was centered on the wall, with a pegboard above it filled with gardening tools. Floor-to-ceiling shelves flanked the bench. Plants lined the shelves with scents ranging from sweet to earthy.

To my right, the wall had a curtain covering the space in between two large armoires. Bookshelves held books with faded bindings on the wall in front of me. Frames containing runes and poems surrounded the shelf.

"What's through the curtains?" I asked.

"That's the old shop." Evangeline pulled the curtains back, revealing a set of French doors. "For decades we had a store—"

"A shop for witches?" I interrupted as I tried to peer through the door panes. A film of dust covered the windows so I couldn't see inside.

"Yes, and for people in need." Luella pulled the curtains back over the doors. "We offered plants, candles, brick dust, and other supplies our fellow witches needed. But we also served non-witches."

"It was wonderful when the shop was open." Evangeline ran her hand over a row of books. "Our coven helped so many with tarot readings, tea leaf reading, potions, and spells."

"So the living came here when they needed help from the dead? Did the dead come here, too?" I glanced around the room, wondering what everything was used for.

"Many came to us on their own, but others needed to be called here. It's easier to perform rituals in the safety of the mansion," Luella said.

"If the shop is closed, how do you help people now? Or have you stopped?" I said.

"Soon, you'll be able to spot the poor souls who need our help." Evangeline put her arm around me and led me back to the center table. "We help those we see, but it was easier when we had a sacred place to do it."

"Before you ask, the store closed when your mother left. She was the heart and soul of our work. When she left, no one wanted to continue." Luella picked up the candelabra. "Let's go outside to the fountain so we can perform the ritual. It's time to look to our future, not our past."

Evangeline handed me the wooden box, and she picked up the bowl with the jasmine flowers. I followed them out the door into the courtyard.

"Are we allowed out here?" I stared at the water fountain as the image of Chloe's body flashed before my eyes.

"Yes, Knox released the courtyard at five this morning." Luella placed the candelabra on the edge of the fountain. "I did a ritual to cleanse the area and said a prayer for Chloe."

"Was Chloe here?" Evangeline asked.

"No, her spirit was not here. Hopefully, she has passed through the veil." Luella wiped a tear from her face.

Evangeline hugged Luella. "I'm sure she's in the afterlife, Lulu. You know Caroline was there to welcome her with open arms."

My heart broke for these women who lost someone who meant a lot to them. I gave them a moment to themselves and strolled over to the side of the courtyard, where the jasmine bloomed. Inhaling the sweet fragrance and touching the soft petals calmed my nerves. I couldn't believe a murder was committed in such a peaceful place.

"Are you ready, Thea?" Evangeline grasped my hand, startling me. "Oh, I didn't mean to scare you."

I squeezed her hand back without thinking, which also surprised me. No one ever made me feel so comfortable so soon.

"I guess I'm ready. Is this going to hurt?" I said.

Evangeline led me toward the fountain. "Sugar, it won't hurt physically. But you will feel overwhelmed when your abilities come back to you. We'll be here for you, and that includes everyone in our coven."

I had a knot in my stomach as we headed to Luella. It dissipated when we stood in front of the fountain. I had no idea what waited for me, but I was ready.

"We do this out in the open?" I said.

They arranged the candelabra, the bowl, and the box around the fountain. I stood by the box, Luella by the candelabra, and Evangeline by the bowl.

"Of course not! We always do a spell so no one can see us," Luella scoffed. She took water from the fountain and let it drip from her hand. "Let us be invisible to the world as we perform our sacred spell. Keep us safe from prying eyes until we are ready to reveal our true selves."

"Now we're protected, and no one can see us," Evangeline said.

Before I did any ridiculous chants, I wanted to see if Luella was serious. "How does it work? The courtyard looks the same."

"Walk five feet from where you're standing, and then look back." Luella sighed. "Go on."

I walked away as she said. The women disappeared when I turned around. The water fountain was the only thing there, and all I heard was the water flowing down the tiers.

I searched for a projector or an explanation for the new image. I twisted a piece of my hair so hard that I yelped.

"Fine. You got me." I returned to my spot where the women and the objects waited.

"Child, when we do this ritual, you better finally believe in magic. Let's not wait any longer."

Luella gave each of us a small booklet. It reminded me of a church hymn book. I flipped it open to find blank pages.

"Why do I have a blank book?" I said.

"It won't be blank for long. As soon as we finish the ritual, you'll be able to read your grimoire," Luella said.

"Grimoire?" I said.

"It's a spellbook. You're holding your own copy. Once you can see it, you'll find our coven's spells and ones you have created," Evangeline said.

"As a six-year-old, I made up spells?" I closed the book shut and considered throwing it in the fountain. If I did that, would my chances of being a witch go away? What was I saying? Did I believe I would gain some magical powers?

No time like the present to find out. What's the worst that could happen? I'd say some silly words, and life would go back to normal.

"Althea, stop moving, and put your grimoire in front of you," Evangeline whispered. "You need to pay attention and open your heart and mind to the ritual."

I surprised myself by putting the book gently down on the fountain, clasping my hands, and standing still. I was speechless and couldn't come up with a sarcastic reply. Was I really going through a "witch renewal" ceremony? Did I believe it would work? No, but these women did. The least I could do was patiently sit through their hocus-pocus.

"My fellow witches, we are here today to reunite Althea Rose Fontenot with her birthright. Our sister needs her powers restored, and we ask our ancestors to help us." Luella's voice was soft but firm. "Althea, please open the wooden box and place the three crystals in front of you. Then you can take out the locket."

The water gurgled out of the fountain, rushing down the center like a river. I expected the fountain to overflow, but it just lapped the edges. I opened the wooden box and took out three pointy-shaped crystals in colors of pink, black, and blue. As Luella asked, I then removed the locket. It was a duplicate of the coven necklace.

"Althea, this is your great-great-great-great-great grandmother's locket. Florence Fontenot formed our coven here in this courtyard in 1850. It is her wisdom, strength, and kindness that guides us to this day," Evangeline said.

The locket had the Fontenot name engraved on the back, like my mother's necklace. I traced the jasmine design on the front with my finger, imagining all the women in my family touching this same locket. A sense of peace came over me. All my life I wondered about my past, and I now held it in my hands.

"As you hold the necklace, reflect on the women who came before us. Once again, you will have the abilities you were born with and those that you learned." Luella took a box of matches out of her pocket. She lit the candles and then blew out the match. The flames flickered, and instead of the smoke blowing straight up, it came toward me.

Luella put her hand over the white candle. "This candle will bring back your witchcraft knowledge. Let its power heal your past and restore your abilities."

"This candle is to strengthen your intuition. Let its powers restore your telepathy and connection to the magical world." Luella moved her hand over the brown candle and then to the purple one. "This candle is to regain your hidden knowledge and memories. Let its power restore and protect your abilities as a Fontenot witch."

As Luella blew out each candle, my body felt weightless,

as if I could float away at any moment. But I could feel my feet firmly connected to the ground.

Evangeline came over to me and picked up the pink crystal. "Rose quartz will help you receive the coven's unconditional love. Let its power restore the harmony in your heart, mind, and soul."

"Hematite will bring forth your inner strength and courage. Let its power restore your confidence in your magical powers." Evangeline added the black crystal to her hand with the rose quartz stone. She picked up the last stone. "Celestine is here to rid you of any anger and negativity you may have toward the loss of your powers. Let its power restore your compassion and connect you to the spirits."

She placed the crystals back down and returned to her place around the fountain. I unclasped my hands to rub my temples. A dull ache formed across my forehead, and my throat went dry. It was as if I had a hangover from a night of too much champagne. I gulped in the cool air and my pain disappeared.

Evangeline took the jasmine flowers out of the bowl and placed them in the bottom tier of the fountain. The flowers bobbed in the water until the water fountain stopped flowing. A breeze came through and blew the jasmine in front of me. They stayed there as if something was holding them in place. Their intoxicating scent filled the air as if the flowers had taken over the courtyard.

Luella and Evangeline spoke in unison, but I didn't understand their words. It was like I was swimming underwater and the women were on the pool deck, speaking to me. Their voices changed in tone and pace for at least five minutes.

My head cleared like I had come to the surface of the

water. The only sounds were the water in the fountain and my own heavy breathing.

"Althea Rose Fontenot, open your eyes. Look at your grimoire," Luella said.

Just as they had promised, the grimoire now had the words *The Fontenot Coven* on the cover. I flipped through the pages, and they were filled with words and illustrations of plants, crystals, and tarot cards. The last page with writing said, "Flowers Big and Small."

Evangeline stood next to me and pointed at the spell. "We did it until our moms stopped us."

With my book in my hands, I walked to the jasmine vines. After clearing my throat, I read the spell. I dropped the book as I reached out to touch the large flowers. I inhaled the calming scent of the jasmine, which was stronger now that they were large. The flowers shrank when I did the reverse incantation spell. Laughing, I picked my book up and held it to my chest.

I was a witch.

16

I returned to the water fountain and Evangeline hugged me. Luella grasped both of my hands and kissed me on the cheek.

"What are you worried about, Luella?" I asked.

"You're reading my mind already?" Luella's eyes twinkled, but I recognized the concern in them.

"I am, and you're still worried about me. Just tell me, please," I said.

"We weren't able to release all your powers." Luella pursed her lips. "I'm not sure why Fern did that. I'm worried that you aren't as strong as you need to be."

"How strong do I need to be?" The joy of becoming a witch was fading fast.

"Since you are the oldest witch in your bloodline, you are the greatest source of our energy," Luella said. "The well could run dry, so to speak."

The fountain gurgled as if it agreed with Luella.

"So if I don't have all my powers, you don't need me?" My cheeks burned, and I went to leave, but Evangeline put her arm around me.

"No, Thea, of course we need you! You're one of us." Evangeline gently tightened her grip on my shoulder.

"Our powers grow stronger as we age. Betty and Donna were two of our strongest witches, as they were the oldest in their family line. Your mother wasn't as old as they were, but as the oldest of the Fontenot family, she was the strongest of the entire coven," Luella explained.

"But she wasn't here but once a year. That was enough for her to be the strongest witch?"

"Her yearly visits kept the magic flowing. She performed a family ritual that invigorates our coven's powers. Since the spell has never been written, only she knew it," Evangeline said.

"What happens without the spell?" I asked.

"We will still be witches, but our abilities to help the living and the dead will be weakened," Luella said. "But I believe the real issue is the loss of the lockets."

"Why do you say that? Can another witch use the locket?" I said.

"Possibly, but we could account for all our lockets until Donna's locket was taken when she died," Luella said.

"But you said mine was missing, and you didn't know where it went."

"Yes, but we weren't too concerned with one locket missing, especially since you were only six and didn't have your full powers yet," Luella said.

"So now that there are two missing, you think the witches are being killed for the lockets? But you don't know why they'd want them." My head ached again.

"That's true," Luella agreed. "The killer could kill for our lockets, to reduce the number of witches in our covens, or even to scare us."

"It could even be for revenge," Evangeline said. "Or to take over our principal mission."

"You mean refereeing for the living and the dead?" I said.

"We have stopped humans and paranormals alike who have tried to mess with the balance between the living and the dead," Evangeline said.

"Great, so we could have humans, witches, or other paranormals beings trying to kill us for our lockets, to get rid of the coven, or to take over the world. You should have led with that information before you turned me back into a witch."

"Don't be a smarty-pants, Althea," Luella snapped.

"I am just telling it like I see it. We don't know why this is happening and without all my powers, I can't help." Becoming a witch was more complicated than I had imagined.

"Your return to the coven is helpful. I promise," Evangeline said as Luella nodded. "But you're right. We're not sure why this is happening and what will happen next."

Despite my initial anger, the concern and love in the women's eyes calmed me.

"Okay, so I need my complete powers to find out what's going on."

"Exactly. With your skills, combined with the rest of us, it will enable us to build up our defenses and to discover who is doing this to us." Luella wiped a stray tear from her face. "I don't want to lose anyone else."

"We won't. How do I get all my powers back?"

"You'll need to ask Fern," Luella said.

"Hold it. I can speak to my mother?" My heart started racing. Forget making flowers bloom. I wanted to talk to my mother.

"Yes, we can see and speak to the dead when they present themselves to us," Luella said.

"So my mother has to come to me? I doubt she'll do that," I said.

"It's possible to summon someone from the afterlife," Evangeline said.

"It's true, but Fern won't be happy about it," Luella said.

"My mother won't be happy that I'm even in this city, never mind the fact you restored my powers. Luella, please tell me how to do it," I pleaded.

"She needs to do this," Evangeline said.

Luella relented. "Did you bring your mother's ashes with you like I asked?"

"I brought some. The rest I scattered into the Puget Sound as she requested in her will." I hadn't planned to keep any of my mother's ashes, but when Luella told me to, I did it. The funeral home put the ashes in a small silver urn that fit into my purse.

"You'll need to take your mother's ashes and your spellbook to your family tomb. When you're there, follow the directions on page fifty-five," Luella said. "But first, we need to bring everything inside."

We gathered the ritual items and headed to the storeroom. Tasso jumped over the courtyard wall and stopped in front of me.

"You're a full-fledged witch again, ain't you?"

"I guess I am. Sorry, but I still don't remember you from my childhood," I said.

"Your momma still has ahold of that, I bet."

"She does, but I'm going to fix that. I'm going to my family's tomb. I don't know where it is, though. I better go ask." I headed inside to find Luella.

"St. Louis Cemetery No. One is where your family's tomb

is at. I'll take you there." Tasso ran out in front of me. "I tell you what, it's going to be a doozy of a family reunion. Better brace yourself for Hurricane Fern."

"My mother should brace herself for Hurricane Althea, actually. I have a lot of questions, and I doubt she's ready for them." I hoped by acting strong that I'd feel that way when I confronted my mother. Assuming this witch ritual worked.

"It's goin' be a Fujiwhara for sure."

"A what?" I asked.

"The Fujiwhara effect is where two hurricanes collide. The stronger one absorbs the smaller one. I wonder which one you'll be."

Tasso trotted up the stairs to the kitchen door. I stared at this strange, orange fat cat in awe. This Cajun talking cat was an expert in meteorology and a tour guide. No one seemed normal around here. And now that included me as I prepared to take a spell book and an urn of ashes to a cemetery to talk to my mother.

17

"Before we head over to St. Louis No. One, let me give you a little history." Tasso stood on the sidewalk as I walked down the front stairs. "Now, this place is called number one because there are two more St. Louis cemeteries. Number two is right behind number one, but number three is over yonder in Bayou St. John. Now, don't let the name fool ya. It's more of a lake than a bayou, in my humble opinion, but that's neither here nor there."

I tried to concentrate on Tasso's history lesson, but his Cajun accent grew thicker the more he spoke. Before I could get him back on track, and have him direct me to the cemetery, Tasso's tail grew bushy and stood up.

"What's wrong?" I followed Tasso's stare and tried to figure out what had upset him. The sidewalks and streets were empty except for a beige sedan that was parked in the middle of the street. Knox emerged from the driver's side door.

"Sorry, Thea-Bea, but this is my cue to vamoose. The lawman and I have history that I don't want to repeat." Tasso

84

ran off in the opposite direction before I could question him.

"Ms. Fontenot, I'm glad I caught you. Could you come with me to the police station?" There was no question in the tone of his voice; this was a command.

"Yes, of course." The warm weather, which I found comfortable yesterday, now felt oppressive. A bead of sweat ran down my back.

"There's nothing to worry about. We just need you to make an official statement at the station. I wanted to offer you a ride." Knox opened the passenger front door.

"Of course." I forced a smile and entered the car. After buckling my seatbelt, I gripped my hands together tightly so they wouldn't shake. I was innocent, but there was something disconcerting about sitting in a police car. At least I was sitting in the front seat and not in the back in handcuffs. Hopefully, I would leave the police station the same way.

In less than fifteen minutes, we had gone from Fontenot Mansion to the French Quarter police station. I was expecting to go to a plain office building, but we entered a two-story yellow building lined with white columns. The grand architecture didn't continue into the interview room. If I hadn't noticed the large mirror—presumably one-way— on the wall facing me, I would have asked if we were in a storage room. The rectangular, silver metal table and matching chairs had dents and scrapes. A beige four-drawer filing cabinet stood in one corner, and stacks of unlabeled file boxes filled the other three corners.

"Are you sure you wouldn't like coffee or water?" Knox asked after he settled into the chair across from me.

"No, thank you." After he poured a cup from an industrial-sized coffee maker, I passed. The bitter aroma made my nose twitch.

"Well, let's get to it." Knox tapped a finger on the manila folder in front of him. "I spoke with the members of the coven. You made quite the impression when you arrived yesterday."

Now I wished I had accepted his offer of water. My throat felt dry and scratchy. "It was mutual. I was overwhelmed meeting them."

"You and Chloe fought."

"We had words, I'll admit. She wasn't welcoming, especially considering she was in my family home." I realized how harsh that sounded as soon as I said it. "I'm sure Chloe was surprised that I was there. My family hasn't lived in the house for over forty years."

"I understand your mother came to visit once a year. She and Chloe fought, too."

"They did? I didn't know my mother came to New Orleans after we moved away."

Knox took a sip of his coffee and made a face. "Good thing you didn't accept my offer for coffee. It's extremely pungent today."

"So the cliché is true. Coffee is bad at police stations," I said.

"It's true. Now tell me if this statement is true. You now own the Fontenot Mansion and are planning to sell it. Was Chloe stopping you?"

Knox asked this as casually as he had commented on the coffee. If he was trying to shake me up, it didn't work. He had no idea how many mystery books I read and how many mystery shows I watched.

"Chloe had no legal standing to keep me from selling my

house as far as I know. Last night was the first time I met her. There is no reason for me to want her dead." I tapped my finger on his manila folder. "Unfortunately, our first meeting didn't go well, but I didn't wish her harm."

"Where did you go after your argument with Chloe?"

"I went inside to get my purse and then went out to get food. Do you want my receipt?" I reached for my purse and took out my wallet.

"Thank you." Knox accepted the receipt and studied it. "You were there at 5:04 p.m. You and Miss Lulu found Chloe at approximately 6:40 p.m. What were you doing between the time you left the shop and returning to your home?"

Should I tell him about Trent the mugger? Actually, he was Trent, the vampire. And then there was Atlas...

"Miss Fontenot? Do you have an answer?" Knox interrupted my internal monologue.

"S-sorry, yes," I stuttered. "I ran into a man who offered to help me with my groceries, but Luella showed up."

"Let me guess, it was Trent?"

"How did you know?"

"We're familiar with Trent's illegal activities. I imagine Miss Lulu showed up just in time, and she called for Atlas McCarthy."

"Are you psychic, too? Or does this happen all the time in this strange town?" I stared at the one-way mirror in the hope that someone would come rushing through the door and say this was all a joke. But it didn't happen.

Knox let out a hearty laugh. "No, I'm not psychic. Miss Lulu is protective of her flock. And whenever Trent gets in trouble, Atlas takes care of it. Those vampires stick together."

"You know they're vampires?"

"Yes, and I know you're a witch. As I said last night, we're very tolerant of the unusual here. But I meant what I said, that murder isn't acceptable no matter what kind of paranormal being you might be." Knox loosened his collar. "Did you want to file a report against Trent?"

"No. I'd rather forget it."

"Good, because it wouldn't do any good. The vampires only come out at night, and they disappear from the cells if we bring them in. It makes for more paperwork than I care for."

Was he joking? I tried to read his mind, but I didn't know how to do it. I needed to read my spellbook.

"Do you know how Chloe died yet?" I asked. "Was it poison?"

"We don't have that information yet. Are you familiar with poisons?"

"Only what I've read in mysteries."

"You don't keep a garden at home?" Knox said.

"No, I have a black thumb, not a green one."

"You don't garden? Isn't that unusual for a witch?" Knox scribbled in his notebook.

"I don't garden, and yes, I've heard it's strange for a witch to kill plants. Is there anything else?" I said.

"Yes, I realize you only met the coven yesterday, but did you notice anyone arguing with Chloe?"

"You're right, I did just meet them, so I doubt I can add anything."

"Ms. Fontenot, I am aware of Chloe's disparaging remarks about Lauren Shaw. There's no need to protect her, so can you tell me what you saw and heard?"

Although I'd just met the women yesterday, I felt a sense of loyalty to them now. Was that because Luella broke my mother's spell? Whatever the case, if Knox knew about the incident with Lauren, I had no reason to deny it. I gave him the details of the conversation, hoping that I wasn't throwing Lauren under the proverbial bus.

"I can't imagine Lauren or anyone killing Chloe over insults. From what I can tell, the coven sticks together no matter what," I said.

"There can be an exception to the rule. Lauren might have just had enough. Did she seem that angry?" Knox said.

"I just met her yesterday! How could I know what level of anger she showed?" I exhaled, blowing the wisps of my hair out of my face. "Surely, you're looking at people outside of the coven. From the article I read in today's paper, Chloe was involved in many clubs and had a large group of friends."

"From your observations yesterday, I assumed you knew that most murders are committed by the people closest to the victim." Knox raised his eyebrows. "Did you miss that episode of *Murder She Wrote*?"

"I see you're a comedian and a detective." I raised my eyebrows at Knox.

"Touché, Ms. Fontenot." Knox pushed back his chair and stood up. "And as they say in those mystery shows, please don't leave town. More importantly, don't investigate Chloe's murder on your own."

"No problem. I have enough to do without playing detective."

"Keep it that way." Knox opened the door and gestured for me to leave.

Whether it was old-fashioned intuition or my new witch senses, I doubted I'd forget about Chloe's death. I was already in the middle of it, apparently still as a suspect. I needed to fix that, but first I needed to talk to my dead mother.

18

I left the police station and decided I was finally ready to eat. Next door was Café Beignet. The sweet scent of powdered sugar wafted out of the restaurant, but I decided against it. As much as I loved pastries, I needed something more substantial. I needed all the energy I could get before going to the cemetery.

There had to be a sandwich shop somewhere on my way to the cemetery, so I started walking along Royal Street. I didn't make it half a block when I heard someone call my name. Across the street, Lauren, the witch Chloe insulted last night, waved at me.

"Hi, Miss Althea! Hold on." Lauren dashed across the street, barely avoiding a delivery truck. She ignored the driver's frustrated gesture and came up to me. "I just wanted to see how you were. Your first day back here has been strange."

"That's an understatement," I said.

"It'll get even stranger now that you have your powers back." Lauren smiled.

"You know about that?" I asked.

"Yes, Miss Evangeline is getting the word out. I've never seen her so happy."

I smiled back at Lauren. I couldn't deny I appreciated how excited Luella and Evangeline were after the ritual. Lauren seemed happy, too. But she seemed anxious as she bit at her already bitten nails.

"How are you holding up? It must be difficult losing a friend," I said.

Lauren dropped her hand from her mouth. "She wasn't a friend. She was a bully. But Chloe was a sister because of the coven, so I put up with her."

"It sounds like you didn't have a choice."

"I guess not. But I don't want to talk about her. Where are you going?" Lauren said.

"I'm going to the cemetery, but first I need lunch. Any suggestions?"

"How about the Gumbo Shop? It's not far from here. I could use something warm on this cold day."

"Cold? This is warm to me." Seventy degree weather felt like a heat wave to me, especially in February. It's all relative, I guess.

"Gumbo is good in any kind of weather. I promise," Lauren said.

"Lead the way." Hopefully, my lunch would come with some information. I'd told Knox I wouldn't play detective, but learning about the victim wouldn't hurt, would it?

I tried to focus on small talk Lauren made as we walked down Royal Street, but it proved difficult. There was so much to see. I lost count of the number of art galleries selling landscape and abstract paintings, unusual sculptures, and photographs. Antique shops showcased elegant furniture and chandeliers while brightly colored souvenir T-shirts appeared to be the best sellers in the gift stores.

Restaurants, coffee shops, and residences filled the spaces in between.

Bands and solo performers entertained enthusiastic crowds on the street corners. I didn't recognize the songs, but I enjoyed them just the same. My body and soul relaxed with each song full of upbeat tempos and soulful voices.

We turned left onto St. Peter Street and joined the line waiting outside the Gumbo Shop. The restaurant's facade was a deep beige with two windows flanking a large door that was blocked by a table from the inside. The line moved quickly, and we passed under a rustic wooden sign hanging above us that read "Gumbo Shop, Creole Cuisine." We entered, what I recognized from Fontenot Mansion, the former carriageway of the building. Straight in front of us was the courtyard, but we were seated in the main dining room. They arranged the tables in a tight space, but the twenty-foot-high ceilings created a feeling of airiness. Large landscape murals covered the walls and overhead fans cooled the room.

"I assume you recommend the gumbo," I said to our server.

"Oh, yes ma'am. They're all good, but I love the chicken-and-andouille-sausage gumbo. It's even better with a strawberry daiquiri," he said.

"It's a little early for a daiquiri for me," I said.

"Not in New Orleans, ma'am! You can drink whenever you want here and no one's going to bat an eyelash. I promise." Our server insisted, but Lauren and I ordered a diet soda along with the chicken-and-sausage gumbo.

"You can order a drink. I don't mind," I said after the server left.

"I have to go to work at two, and showing up tipsy wouldn't be good."

"Where do you work?" I broke off a piece of bread from a basket on the table and smothered it with butter. The crunchy bread and the rich butter melted in my mouth. I wanted to eat all the bread, but I pushed the basket away from me.

"I'm a technician at a pharmacy, but I'm looking for a new job." Lauren reached for the bread basket, but pulled her hand back.

"You don't like the job?"

"I do, but they complain I spend too much time talking to the customers."

"I'm sure the customers appreciate your concern for them," I said.

"They do, but I wish the coven had a place where we could help people. Not everyone needs pills. You wouldn't believe how much medication there is out there." Lauren stopped eyeing the bread basket and took out a piece.

"As a technician, do you make up prescriptions?"

"I do, but it's not my favorite part. Why do you ask? Do you think I stole pills to kill Chloe? Is that how she died?" Lauren dropped her piece of bread on her plate and her face turned red.

Before I spoke, the server returned with our sodas. When he left, I said, "The detective told me they don't know how she died yet. I'm sorry, Lauren, I didn't mean to upset you."

"After last night, I'm suspect number one. The detective hinted I was when I talked to him today. I'm not a killer."

"Of course you're not." My stomach gurgled from hunger but also from distress. I didn't want to upset Lauren, but she had a motive and the means to kill Chloe. I needed to learn to ask questions subtly if I wanted anyone to keep talking to me.

Lauren gave me the same annoyed look that my daughter gave me when she said I was being patronizing. She spread an entire pat of butter on her small piece of bread and shoved it in her mouth.

"Don't worry, the police asked me if I killed Chloe, and I just met her yesterday. I think everyone is a suspect." I turned to the server, who placed our food on the table. "Thank you."

"If you change your mind about a daiquiri, just holler," he said.

I considered calling him back, but alcohol wasn't the answer. "Lauren, I'm sorry. This is a horrible situation."

"It's okay. I feel better that you're a suspect, too. I'm in good company, I guess." Lauren gave a slight smile and picked up her spoon to eat.

Judging by the line, the food must be great. Staring at the bowl in front of me, I wasn't so sure. The dark brown soup had a clump of rice in the center. Why wasn't it mixed in?

I dipped my spoon into the soup and swirled it around. There was chicken and sausage and okra. I braced myself for a funky taste, but once again I was surprised. The rich taste of vegetables, chicken, and sausage delighted my taste buds. The rice made sense now; it was a cooling break from the earthy spiciness of the soup.

"You really like gumbo, don't you?"

I lifted my head to find Lauren staring at my bowl. Half of the soup was already gone. "I haven't eaten until now. Sorry, I didn't mean to be rude."

Lauren smiled. "You're not rude. It's nice to go out with someone who enjoys food. My friends order salads and just pick at them."

"My daughter had a few friends like that in high school, but most were like her. Olivia would love this soup."

"Your daughter is lucky." Lauren broke off a piece of bread and dipped it into her bowl.

"Good friends aren't always easy to find." I took a sip of my drink. "Is it safe to say Chloe wasn't part of your friend group?"

"I avoided her as much as possible, which suited her just fine. Chloe wanted friends who accepted everything she said and were pretty like her. Well, not as pretty, since she didn't want any competition."

"With that attitude, I imagine she had a lot of enemies," I said. "Was Chloe as dedicated as you to the coven?"

Lauren picked up her spoon and began eating again. The food had a calming effect on her, and she spoke in between mouthfuls. "Chloe loved being a witch, but not for the right reasons. Our gifts should make the world better. Chloe always pushed her ideas."

"What ideas did she have?"

"She said we should use our relationship with the dead to learn about the living. Chloe claimed it would help those in need, but I bet she wanted the information for blackmail. Money was always on her mind." Lauren scrunched up her face. "Power and money made her happy, and I wouldn't be surprised if that's what killed her."

Lauren continued with her meal, allowing me to consider her words. Could Chloe's murder result from a blackmail scheme? Or did another witch finally tire of Chloe's push to change the coven?

"Is there anything else that might help me find out who killed Chloe?" I asked.

"Are you a detective? Luella told us you were here to rejoin the coven."

"No, I'm not a detective." I laughed, hoping to lighten the mood. "Having an unsolved murder hanging over the coven won't help any of us, so I just thought I'd ask a few questions."

"I bet you watch those true crime shows like my mom."

"I prefer the fictional ones better, but yes, I enjoy mysteries." I smiled.

"Since you know how I feel about Chloe, do you want my information?"

"Yes, I do. I need help to understand life in the coven."

"Okay, but you didn't hear this from me." Lauren scooted her chair closer to the table and lowered her voice. "Luella told me you met Trent and Atlas, the vampires. Atlas is quiet, but nice. Trent is not."

"I agree with you. Did Chloe hang around with vampires? Was she dating one?"

Lauren smirked. "Chloe wouldn't stoop to dating a blood sucker. Those are her words, not mine. But I saw her hanging around with Trent a few times."

Considering my first interactions with Chloe and Trent were negative, it didn't surprise me the two of them were friendly. "Did you ever confront her about it?"

"No, but Luella did. She reminded Chloe that we don't date vampires, and Chloe got real defensive. Of course, she was always defensive if anyone told her she was doing something wrong." Lauren rolled her eyes. "Chloe claimed Trent bothered her, and she wanted nothing to do with him."

"But you didn't believe her, did you?" I said.

"No, especially when I saw them outside the bar, Dusk. I couldn't hear what they were saying, but it seemed intense, by their faces."

"What do you think they were up to?"

"Whatever it was, I bet it wasn't good. The Bordelon Coven hangs out there when they're in town," Lauren said.

"Tell me about the Bordelon Coven."

After our server refilled our sodas, Lauren explained that there were several covens in the area. Each was named after their founding family and had their own special gifts.

"Our gift is helping the living and the dead. The Bordelon Coven is known for their ability to heal animals, particularly those that live in the bayou," Lauren said. "Like us, they're also good with plants and performing psychic readings and cleanses."

"They sound fine, but by the tone of your voice, you have a problem with them."

"I do, and so does most of our coven. We're polite, but there's tension because of the 'incident.'" Lauren used air quotes.

"What incident?"

Lauren's face went pale. "I just stuck my foot in my mouth. I forgot your mom was part of that ritual."

"It's fine, Lauren. I know nothing about my mother's time in the coven, so I want to hear everything." I looked her straight in the eye, hoping she would keep talking.

"Well, okay. Chloe's grandmother and a Bordelon witch helped your mother in some ritual. You know your mom was the only one who came back alive, right?"

"I do. What I don't know is what ritual they were doing," I said.

"I'm not sure of the details, but it had to do with crossing the veil—"

"Crossing the veil?"

"You know, going to the afterlife, the land of the dead. We're not supposed to go there."

"But I thought we were supposed to help the dead with their problems," I said.

"Yes, we can talk to them, but we're not supposed to enter their world physically. And before you ask, I don't know what they were doing. All I know is your mom was the only survivor." Lauren grabbed the last piece of bread and shoved it into her mouth.

Again, I considered calling our server over for a daiquiri. But considering I needed to go speak with my dead mother at a cemetery, I didn't. Instead, I signaled the server and asked about dessert.

"Pecan pie with extra whipped cream and two spoons, please," I said.

Lauren checked her phone while we waited for the dessert. I hated when Olivia did it, but I'd come to terms that her generation thought of their phone as their lifeline. I couldn't deny that I enjoyed playing crossword puzzles on mine when I was waiting for an appointment. But I suspected Lauren used her phone so she wouldn't have to speak. But after our dessert arrived, I began my questions again.

"So after the ritual, our relationship with that coven was strained. Are we friendly with other covens?" I said, after finishing a bite of the pie. The sugar from it and the whipped cream were just the boost of energy I needed to finish this conversation.

"Yes, we are, but the Bordelon Coven isn't. They're not in the city, but they have a shop here in the Quarter called Teas, Tarots, and Truths," Lauren said.

"Is that where Chloe got her tea?"

"Maybe. That might explain why it smelled. The Bordelon Coven makes unusual teas and they sell crystals and offer tarot readings, too. Are you going to finish that?" Lauren had her spoon raised over my last bite of pie.

"It's all yours. Thanks for talking to me, Lauren. I appreciate it." I signaled the server for our check. Not only did I discover I liked gumbo, I had more information about Chloe, my mother, and witches.

I didn't want to, but I had to consider Lauren a suspect. But now I had two new suspects: Trent and the Bordelon Coven. I'd look into them, but first I couldn't put it off any longer. It was time to talk to my mother.

19

———

"Thanks for lunch, Althea. I'll see you tonight at the house—actually your house."

Lauren gave me a quick hug and headed off to her job. I pulled out my phone and put in the address for St. Louis Cemetery No. 1. My legs felt heavy as I headed on St. Peter Street toward Rampart Street. I was never good at confronting my mother when she was alive. Would I be any better at it now she was dead?

I tried to put it out of my mind as I walked slowly toward my destination. Fortunately, the Mardi Gras decorations were a pleasant distraction. Purple, green, and gold were everywhere and on everything. I had never encountered so many lights, flags, and wreaths, apart from Halloween or Christmas. And then there were the bead necklaces. Bead necklaces were scattered over fences, gaslights, and even trees. Seattle had nothing on New Orleans when it came to celebrating a holiday.

I turned left on Rampart Street, which turned out to be a four-lane divided road. My city skills came in handy as I raced across the road in between the fast cars on both sides.

I wished I hadn't dropped wine on my shoes the other night, as my black flats were already giving me blisters. I wondered if my grimoire included a spell for cleaning or blisters. My mother might have one since her shoes were always clean, even when she was gardening. But I shouldn't waste time thinking about dirty shoes. I had more important questions to ask.

I reached the front gate of the cemetery to find a gaggle of tourists waiting to get inside. People pay to go into a graveyard? Luella said I didn't have to pay since my family owned a mausoleum, so I got in line to tell the guard. Something brushed my legs, making me jump.

"Tasso! You scared me." The talking cat wove in and out of my legs to the oohs and awws of the tourists in line.

"Is this your cat? Did he follow you here?" asked a man wearing a NOLA baseball hat and holding a map in his hand.

"Yes, he did. I better take him home." I picked up Tasso and walked up to and around the next corner before setting him down.

"You could have let me walk." Tasso cleaned his face after giving me a dirty look.

"Sorry, but I figured people would think I was drunk if I talked to a cat. When you answered, they would have called the cops for sure."

"First, they can't hear me talk. All they hear is meows. And second, no one thinks twice if they see someone talking to themselves here. You shouldn't ignore any paranormal people or animals that talk to you, Thea-Bea."

"Locals may not consider it strange, but tourists would. What are you doing here?"

"I've been waiting around for you, but you took forever. Knox didn't try to arrest you, did he?"

"No, he didn't. Afterward, I ran into Lauren and we had lunch at the Gumbo Shop."

Tasso licked his mouth. "Mmm, I love gumbo. Next time, bring me back the seafood one. I tell you what, nothing is better than shrimp."

"I'll make a note. But why are you here?"

"I figured you might try to go through the front gate if you hadn't read your spellbook. Follow me." Tasso turned right and trotted halfway down the block. I followed him where he waited at a smaller gate than the one in front of the cemetery.

"I don't have a key to this gate," I said.

"Cher, you don't need one. This is the gate for witches. Just get your book out for the unlocking spell on page seventeen."

"Are you a witch, too? You know the spellbook by heart." I took out my grimoire, and sure enough, the unlocking spell was on page seventeen.

"Nope. I'm just your average talking cat."

"You're anything but average."

"I was being modest." Tasso swished his tail back and forth.

I read the spell, "Unlock this door with intentions pure. My purpose is peaceful, and no harm shall come I do ensure." The lock clicked open, and I took it off the chain. The gate opened, and Tasso ran in before I did. I closed it behind me and put the padlock back on so no one else would come in. Well, at least so a non-witch wouldn't enter.

"This way, Thea."

The mausoleums were like nothing I had seen before. Many were elegant white plastered tombs with the family surname engraved on top and a list of the people buried inside, on a plaque. Others were crumbling apart with bricks peeking through the plaster. Weeds sprouted from cracks in the bricks and grew up the sides of the tombs.

I noted a large round building in the distance that must hold a large, family or perhaps it was for an organization. If I wasn't here with a purpose, I would have strolled carefully through the gravel and paved pathways to get to it. Instead I followed Tasso past the other tombs that were smaller. Some were just the height and width of one casket, but most were around eight feet tall by four feet wide. By the long list of names etched on the plaques on the mausoleums, it seemed impossible to put that many bodies in one.

"Tasso, how can they bury so many people in one building?" I asked.

"You don't know? They put the coffin on top of the newest one. They call the tombs 'ovens' here. The heat makes the bodies decompose, and they brush the bones down to the bottom of the tomb."

"Are you kidding me?"

"No. You're not supposed to open a mausoleum for a day and a year after the last burial. Even then, the body might still be soup instead of bones."

I shook my head as I stared at a mausoleum with a long list of names. The first person was buried in 1893 and the last in 1999, so I guess that made sense. But liquid bodies weren't an image I wanted today, or any day.

As we walked past another crumbling mausoleum, it was obvious some of them had been abandoned.

"Tasso, who takes care of my family tomb?"

"Your momma did, so now it's up to you. You should bring fresh flowers, and during Mardi Gras you can leave beads. Honoring your ancestors is the right thing to do."

Sure enough, we passed a tomb with a cherub statue wearing a strand of green beads. A vase of lilies rested on the step of another tomb. Three x's marked in red-brown were on the side of the next tomb.

"Why does that one have that mark on it?" I pointed it out to Tasso.

"That's a Voodoo tradition. People think if they use a brick and draw those x's, Marie Laveau will grant them their wish."

"Sounds like you don't believe in Voodoo," I said.

"I do believe in Voodoo!" Tasso meowed. "They're a powerful group, like the witches. But Marie Laveau won't grant any wishes that way."

"Who is she?"

"She's the Voodoo Queen! You have a lot of history to catch up on, Thea. The witches and the Voodoo community get along, but they don't really mix."

"How does Marie Laveau grant wishes? Do you meet her here, or does she have a church?"

"I don't know how she does it. She's actually dead. Well, they say she's dead, but I have my doubts." Tasso picked up the pace. "Come on, cher, don't dillydally any longer."

I'd rather have spent the afternoon asking Tasso questions, but he was right. I couldn't avoid my mission here any longer. After stepping past more graves and squeezing in between two tombs, Tasso sat in front of a large, white mausoleum. On top of the pitched roof was a statue of a woman with long hair, wearing a locket. Jasmine vines were etched around the top and the sides of the white building and underneath the top vines, it said, "Fontenot." There were two steps, the width of the tomb, that led to a marble plaque bolted to the front. Interestingly, only women where listed on the plaque:

Florence

Born 1827—Died 1897

Anna

Born 1844—Died 1916

Caroline

Born 1870— Died 1945

Mary

Born 1890—Died 1963

Dorothy

Born1912—Died 1964

Iris

Born 1930—Died 1985

Fern

Born 1956—Died 2023

"So, I don't enter this building, do I? Does the plaque cover up where the coffins go?" I ran my hand over the names, stopping at my mother's. Luella must have added my mother's name.

"You got it. Now there are some fancy-pants families who have big mausoleums that you can walk inside, but most of us are practical around here." Tasso put his paw on a flower petal that blew past us. "Are you going to put some of your momma's ashes in here now?"

"No. I'm here to talk to her, assuming she'll come to me."

"I bet she will, but I'll skedaddle before she gets here." Tasso rubbed up against my legs.

Before I could object, Tasso dashed in between the mausoleums and disappeared out of sight. I could have used his moral support, but if I were him, I would have run off, too. I sat on the top step and opened up my spellbook to page fifty-five as Luella told me. With bated breath, I took out the small urn from my purse and began the incantation.

"To Fern Fontenot, ancestor dear, With an open heart, I draw you near. Show your spirit, let us embrace, In separate realms, let's meet face-to-face."

Clouds blocked the sun like a scene from a horror movie. The petals Tasso had played with earlier floated in the air as a gust of wind blew through the row of tombs. For a moment, I thought a white bedsheet blew into the cemetery, but as it drifted toward me, my body shook.

The white sheet turned into the shape of the woman I had cremated a week ago.

My mother had arrived.

20

"Althea Rose Fontenot! What are you doing here?"

My mother stood before me. Although she appeared in white, I recognized the dress and shoes I picked out for her cremation. And I also recognized the angry face she used when berating me as a child and as an adult.

"Hi, to you, too." I folded my arms in part to calm my nerves and to stop myself from reaching out to touch my mother. Hugging her was out of the question. I didn't know if it was physically possible, but when she was this irate, she didn't want anyone within five feet of her.

"I see Lulu broke my spells. Did you accept your witch powers?"

"Yes, Luella undid some of your handiwork. But not all. I still don't remember our time here in New Orleans." I let my arms drop to my sides. Even with the dark clouds and breeze, my body grew hotter the longer I stared at my ghost-mother. "I can't believe you didn't tell me about all of this!"

"I did what I thought was best. Being a witch is hard. Life

isn't any easier with magical powers. It can complicate things."

"So I've heard," I snapped.

"What does that mean?"

"I was told you murdered two other witches, and that's why we left New Orleans. What happened here?"

Although my mother wasn't flesh and blood, I swore her face went pale.

"I told you not to come here. I spelled it out in my will. For once, why didn't you listen to me?" She paced in front of the mausoleum.

"Oh, please, I listened to you all my life! I did everything you asked." I jumped up and tried to block my mother from pacing. Instead, she walked through me. I shivered from the chilly air that trailed after her.

"You did not! I insisted you shouldn't have a child until you had a career and were married!"

"Sorry I followed the family tradition of getting knocked up young and single. I listened to you about not marrying Martin." I crossed my arms to calm myself and to keep them from flailing around. If I acted calm, I hoped I would be calm.

"I'll give you that. Olivia's father had the good sense to let you raise her, and she is a lovely young woman." Fern sat down on the steps of the tomb and wiped a tear from her face. Who knew that ghosts could cry? "I've been watching her now and then and she's so happy in Australia. You haven't told her about this, have you?"

"Which part? That we're witches or you're an accused killer? And now I can add that I'm a murder suspect, too." I should have been kinder since my mother was crying. She never did it in front of me, but all my pent-up anger spilled over into my words.

My mother wiped her eyes and stood up. "What do you mean, you're a murder suspect? You're not talking about Chloe Chase, are you?"

"The very one. Have you seen her? Is she here?"

"Her grandmother and I found her in the afterlife. Chloe is as furious as you are now. This wasn't what she planned for her life."

"I doubt anyone plans to be murdered. Does she say who did it?"

My mother shook her head. "No, but I think she has her suspicions."

"Can you get her here? I need to talk to her."

"She and her grandmother are deep in the afterlife world. Even if you or I called her here, I doubt she'd tell you the truth. Even as a child, Chloe lied. But she didn't deserve to be murdered."

"No one deserves that." I sat next to my mother on the steps. We weren't an affectionate family, but I reached over to grasp her hand. My hand landed on the step instead.

"You'll have to get used to spirits now. You can't touch us, but we can brush by you. Is it cold sitting next to me?" My mother's eyes crinkled as she smiled at me.

"A little. Hold it, are there ghosts in Fontenot Mansion? It's drafty in most of the rooms, except the bathroom."

"Yes, but I'll let Lulu explain that to you. But don't worry, we spirits have manners and won't invade your privacy," she said.

"That's the least of my worries." I gripped my hands together. "I'm a murder suspect in Chloe's death. Until the police solve the case, I doubt they'll let me leave town."

"So you don't plan on staying here? Good." My mother nodded. "Lulu and the coven must be beside themselves. I imagine they've been trying to get you to stay."

"You're right. The coven has lost a few members, and they said I'm the key to its survival."

My mother stood up and paced once again. She twirled a piece of her hair, a habit she always tried to break me of.

"Mom, quit pacing and talk to me," I pleaded.

She stopped and sat back next to me. "The coven thinks as the founders, the Fontenots are the most powerful witches. We aren't. My great-great-great-great-grandmother opened her home to the coven, that's all."

"So we're not special witches?"

"Absolutely not. Lulu and the others are doing just fine without a Fontenot. Don't let them tell you otherwise."

"Oh." Now I caught myself twirling a piece of my hair.

"I see that look in your eye, the one where you're coming up with a big plan. Remember all those plans you made as a teenager? You didn't do any of them. You barely graduated from college and never owned a business of your own."

My mother's sharp tone brought me back to the times she harped on my failures. Rarely did she commend me for the goals I accomplished. But I wasn't here to rehash those moments.

"Mom, I'm searching for the truth. Luella and Evangeline have been far more supportive than you. For once, won't you be honest with me? Tell me why you left and why Luella says someone killed you."

"Forget New Orleans. Visit Olivia, then make your own life. You'll never be a successful witch, so forget what you've learned." My mother floated into the middle of the aisle, out of my reach.

"But Mom..."

"I mean it, Althea. Once you can leave this town, go. You're no help to the coven." She turned her back to me and said, "They don't need you."

My mother disappeared into thin air. Sobs wracked my body as I gathered up her urn and my spellbook. My mother could be blunt, but never this cruel. What gave her the right to question my witching aptitude? Why couldn't I be part of this group of women with special powers? The rest of the coven said I was an important witch.

Who should I believe?

Once my tears subsided, I took a tissue out of my purse and looked at my phone. A text from Evangeline made me smile: *"Let me know when you're done at the cemetery. After meeting with your momma, I know you need a drink, darling."*

A drink was in order. The chill in the air since sunset made the cemetery uncomfortable. The silence bothered me, too. Everything about my surroundings put me on edge.

No one else was in the graveyard since the tours had stopped. I hadn't seen any tourists while talking to my mother. If anyone had come by, they might have guessed that I was grieving the loss of a loved one. Grief would have been easier to handle than these feelings of betrayal and anger.

Fern Fontenot claimed she knew best for me, but now I wanted to prove her wrong. Even if I didn't stay in New Orleans, I would be the best witch I could be.

First, I had to prove I didn't kill Chloe. Second, I needed to find out if my mother had been murdered.

I just wished my mother would help me.

I left the cemetery the way I came and locked the gate behind me. Tasso wasn't waiting for me as I had hoped, but someone else was there.

"Good evening, Althea," Atlas said.

"What are you doing here?" I blurted out as my pulse raced. Sure, finding a vampire waiting for you outside a cemetery was disconcerting, but not because I feared he wanted to bite my neck. His soft voice and compassionate eyes surprised me since we had just met.

"Tasso asked me to escort you home," Atlas said.

"Really? Did he think I couldn't find my way home?" I put my phone back in my pocket. True, I planned to look up directions to Fontenot Mansion, but I didn't need a cat sending a vampire to help me.

"He was concerned about your state of mind after speaking with your mother. Tasso had another engagement, but he wanted to make sure you were all right." Atlas spoke calmly even though I snapped at him.

"Oh, well, that was kind of him. I'm fine," I lied.

"If I may be so bold, you don't appear fine. Between the

tear stains on your face, and the way you're twirling your hair into a knot, you must be upset. Talking with Fern surely was difficult."

Atlas's fingers touched my hand that was twisting my hair. This time, his skin was warm. I stopped twirling my hair, but he didn't remove his hand. We stared at each other like two teenagers who weren't sure what to do next. I recovered my composure and removed my hand.

"You're right. My mother is dead, but we acted like we did when she was alive. The afterlife hasn't softened her at all." I faked a smile. "But I'll be okay."

"People tend to stay the same in death as they were in life. While I'm sure you're fine, may I walk you home?" Atlas offered me his arm.

I threaded my arm through his, letting the warmth of his body and his words comfort me. Tasso knew what I needed, so I would thank him with a bowl of seafood gumbo.

We walked away from the cemetery and crossed Rampart Street.

"Before Tasso roped you into being my escort, what were you doing?" I said.

"I was at my jazz club, Syncopation and Spirits," Atlas said.

"Let me guess, the club is just for paranormals. Unless I'm reading too much into the name." I laughed.

"No, you're right." Atlas smiled, and I noticed his fangs weren't showing. "Syncopation was irresistible to a musician."

"I'm not a musician, but I took piano lessons until I was thirteen. If I recall my stickler of a piano teacher, Miss Burns, syncopation is an interruption of a regular rhythm."

"Yes, that's a simple way of describing it, and a simple

way to describe those in the paranormal realm. But most people assume I named the club just after a music term."

"Is the place only for vampires?"

"No, werewolves, fairies, Voodoo priestesses, and ghosts are welcome. And witches, too, of course."

"Let me guess, humans aren't allowed, to prevent the world from discovering that supernaturals are actually real. I still can't believe I'm saying that."

"I felt the same way until I became a vampire at the ripe old age of forty-seven. After ninety-seven years, I'm used to it."

I stopped walking and looked up at Atlas. "You've been a vampire for ninety-seven years?"

"Yes."

I did the math. Atlas would have become a vampire in 1926. His pained expression kept me from asking him about becoming a vampire. Yes, I was dying to know, no pun intended, but I didn't want to ruin this time with him.

"You're one hundred and forty-four years old, then, if I've added correctly." I studied his face. "Well, you don't look a day over one hundred and forty-three. You must use a fantastic moisturizer."

Atlas's laugh erased all the tension in his face. "Thank you. I'll send your regards to my dermatologist."

We strolled through the Quarter, weaving in and out of crowds of people. We heard laughter and music as we moved away from the cemetery. Plastic cups were a popular accessory since drinking was legal on the streets. Bead necklaces were a close runner-up, with both men and women wearing them.

"Is there a Mardi Gras parade tonight? I've never seen so many people wearing beads," I asked.

"Tourists wear them all year long. The locals do when

they receive them from the parade floats. There are no parades this evening, but in the next few days you can get all the beads you'd like," Atlas said.

Tourists were also easy to spot by the tour-group stickers they wore and their wide-eyed expressions as their guide relayed ghost stories. We were smiling when we heard the guide say, "You never know who you're walking next to in the French Quarter. A vampire could be right here in our midst!"

"Atlas, is there a way to tell if someone has supernatural abilities?" I studied the people passing us.

"As a vampire, I can spot another, even if they're not showing their fangs." Atlas flashed his fangs before retracting them. "I imagine you can spot other witches, or you will soon. You just had your powers restored today from what Tasso told me."

"Tasso has a big mouth and a big belly," I said. "Yes, I did, but not all of them. Luella couldn't break all my mother's spells today."

I tensed as I mentioned my mother. Atlas noticed the change and stopped walking. He took my arm from his and then held my hand. "Althea, families are difficult, no matter who or what we are. Give yourself and your mother a little time. All mothers think they know best, and frequently, they're right."

I bit the inside of my lip not to cry. Discussing my mother wasn't something I wanted to do. I took my hand from Atlas and took my cell phone from my pocket.

"I'm sorry, you must be tired, and I'm keeping you here talking about uncomfortable subjects," Atlas said.

"It's fine. But yes, let's change the subject. I'd love to see your club." I smiled. "Since I'm a witch, I assume you'll let me in."

"I would be delighted."

"Let me text Evangeline that I'll be at the club. She wanted to talk tonight." I texted her I was going to Atlas's club and received a quick response of a smiley face and a winky-smile-face emoji.

Atlas offered his arm again, and I accepted it. "Althea, you must be curious how all paranormals came to be, including me."

"I am, but I have a feeling not everyone, including you, has a happy origin story," I said.

"Origin story? That's an interesting way of putting it." He raised his eyebrows. "It makes us sound like superheroes, which many of us are not, I'm afraid."

"Yes, Trent isn't a hero," I said.

"Trent would cringe if anyone called him a hero. He considers himself a cool cat who lives life to the fullest." Atlas shook his head.

"It must offend Tasso that Trent thinks of himself as a cool cat." I laughed.

"I believe you're right. There's no love lost between those two. Trent doesn't make friends easily."

"Did he act like that before becoming a vampire?"

Atlas sighed. "Our group discovered him wandering around soon after he became a vampire. We took him in and have tried to teach him right from wrong."

"I hate to say I don't think it's worked."

I considered confiding in Atlas that Trent lied when he said he didn't see my necklace, when we met. Before I could decide, Atlas stopped walking and stood in front of a three-story brick townhouse painted a deep green. The second and third floors each had wrought-iron balconies decorated with lush, hanging ferns. Black shutters covered the first-floor windows, and a gate covered the steps leading to the front door.

"I am sorry that Trent was your introduction to vampires. We're not all like him. I promise," Atlas said.

"You've made up for his shortcomings." I felt myself blush, but I realized Atlas was, too. Or could it be the blood was flowing to his face because he had eaten recently?

"Thank you. I hope I can convince you that other paranormals are good, too," Atlas said. "This is my club. Are you ready to go inside?"

I stared at the building. "This is your club? It doesn't look like a business."

"The club takes up the first and second floors. My personal residence is on the third floor. Before you ask, yes, vampires sleep in coffins. It's the safest place for us."

"I'm sure it's more comfortable than the futon I slept in when I was in college." I laughed and looked up at the building, trying to appear casual. Sure, I was curious about other supernatural beings, but Atlas especially.

"Let's go introduce you to the community. Are you ready?" Atlas didn't use the doorbell but unlocked the door with a wave of his hand.

"As ready as I'll ever be." I took in a deep breath and took my first step into the club and the world of the supernatural.

22

"You noticed the doorbell, didn't you? It only rings if a paranormal presses it. If a human tries, it doesn't make a sound and they leave," Atlas said as we stood in the foyer. "And yes, it is a witch spell that makes them leave in haste."

"That makes sense." I had only been a witch for a few hours, but I was already acting like witchcraft was normal. Once a witch, always a witch, I guess.

"Let me show you around." Atlas stopped in front of the first door on the left. "This is the downstairs dining room and lounge. The door farther down leads to a bar and through the bar you can reach the courtyard."

From the noise behind the door, it appeared the rooms were full. I hesitated to look, as I wasn't quite ready to meet anyone. Atlas sensed my nervousness.

"It's all right, Thea. You don't need to go inside until you're ready. Let's go upstairs to the music room. If you're still uncomfortable, we can leave. But I have a feeling you will enjoy the music."

The tension in my shoulders released as I followed Atlas

up the polished staircase to the next floor.

"When you said music room, do you mean it's a small room with a piano in it?" The second floor was eerily silent. Granted, the two doors in the hallway were closed, but I still expected to hear something.

"Ah yes, the silence is surprising." Atlas grinned. "There is another spell here to keep the noise inside the rooms. We don't want it to find its way to the outside world or to the dining room. Why don't you go in first?"

When I opened the door, all my senses went haywire. This was one of the most exciting places I'd been to.

Three walls were covered with a dark gray wallpaper with a tiny, black fleur-di-lis pattern. A large wooden bar with a mirror above it ran the length of the wall in front of me. Patrons had to step up to reach the built-in stools lining the bar. Liquor bottles of all shapes and sizes filled the shelves attached to the mirror.

Through the bottles, the mirror reflected the incredible row of four crystal chandeliers that hung from the center of the room. The chandeliers lit the room in a soft glow, but it was bright enough to see the round tables in varying sizes with chairs covered in green velvet. At the end of the room was a stage with a four-piece band playing jazz.

Those who weren't eating dinner off fine china or drinking from crystal glasses had their eyes focused on the stage. I didn't know the song, but the crowd appeared to, as most sang along and tapped their feet. Naturally, it wasn't a normal band, but one made up of ghosts. The trumpet player, the double-bass player, the pianist, the drummer, and their instruments were all spirits. The upbeat rhythms were just as loud and energetic as if the band consisted of living players. I swayed to the music without thinking; my body just responded to it.

Surprisingly, it was the people inside that caught my attention the most, despite the great music and room. According to Atlas, it was a club for paranormals, and I embarrassingly expected a Halloween costume party. But on the surface, everyone looked normal. Well, except for the group with wings.

"Atlas, I'm sorry to interrupt, but can you help me get more absinthe? The fairies are drinking it like water tonight." The man wore a "Bartholomew" name tag on the black vest he wore over a white shirt.

Laughter erupted from the corner of the room. Three women and three men were gathered around a table filled with glasses. While they were all dressed in normal clothes, there were wings attached to their backs. Watching the fairies flap their wings at various speeds was mesmerizing. When one of them looked at me, I turned away. Staring, especially as a newcomer, wouldn't be good for me, I assumed. And I was right.

"Hey, girlie, whatcha staring at?" One of the male fairies flew over and landed in front of me. "Never seen a fairy before?"

"I'm sorry. I didn't mean to stare. It's my first time here." I had to restrain myself from touching his iridescent wings. They sparkled under the dim light. The wings my daughter wore for her eighth Halloween were plain compared to the ones attached to this man's back.

"Is that so? What are you, then? A werewolf?" The fairy reached out and pulled a strand of my hair. I yelled and stumbled backward against Atlas. He helped me get my balance and then put his hand out to the fairy.

"Gavin, I've told you not to touch anyone without their permission," Atlas said. "Give me the hair."

Gavin handed it to Atlas who then gave it to me. I shoved it in my pocket, since I didn't know what else to do with it.

Gavin stared down at the ground. "Sorry, Atlas. No one new has shown up in a while." Gavin looked back up. "And ma'am, your hair really is beautiful and I couldn't resist."

"Thank you. And yes, I'm new here, and no, I'm not a werewolf. I'm a witch." As soon as I said the words, goosebumps rose on my arms. Saying it out loud was strange, but somehow it felt right. I took the locket and pulled it out from under my shirt and let it rest on my chest.

"Oh, you're a Fontenot witch!" Gavin clapped his hands together like a child receiving a present. "Your coven is great. Y'all have helped the fairy community a lot. But why haven't we seen you?"

At this point, everyone in the room was focused on me. I looked at Atlas, hoping he would help me out, but he just nodded at me. I exhaled and said, "I'm here for a visit. I'm Althea Fontenot."

Gasps and whispers replaced the silence. I made out a few phrases like "That's Fern's daughter!" and "What is she doing here?" I wished a hole in the floor would open and swallow me. The attention made me uncomfortable.

This time, Atlas came to the rescue. "All right, everyone, let's quiet down. Louis and the band will finish soon."

The patrons returned to their conversations and focused on the band. My stomach settled down when I was no longer the center of attention. Gavin bowed and then flew back to his table.

"Atlas, I'll wait for you in the storeroom. If you'll come help me once you get our new guest settled, I'd be grateful. Welcome to the club, Miss Althea." Bartholomew left Atlas and me alone.

"Althea, are you all right? You look a little pale," Atlas

said.

"I'm not used to all this attention." I coughed. My throat ached from dryness. "And I just realized I haven't eaten since lunch. You don't offer food here, do you?"

"Do you like crawfish? Tonight we have a fantastic crawfish étouffée. Or at least that's what the chef tells me," Atlas said. "He's a warlock and can actually eat the food."

"Umm, do you serve food for vampires?" A server walked past with a tray of glasses filled with what I assumed was red wine before Atlas spoke.

"Do you really want the answer to that?" Atlas raised his eyebrows.

"No, I don't. Back to crawfish, I haven't had it before. Is it like lobster?"

"Close enough, as I recall." Atlas pointed toward the stage. "Please take a seat, and I'll have your meal out soon. What would you like to drink?"

"Thanks, and I'd love a glass of wine. White, that is."

Atlas winked and followed his employee through a door marked Private to the left of the bar.

Trying to ignore the stares of the surrounding people, I wove in between the tables toward an empty one to the left of the stage. Before I reached the table, I recognized Knox sitting by himself. His back was toward me, but I knew it was him from his suit and the thick, wavy hair. Maybe with a drink or two in him, Knox would tell me more about the investigation. It was a long shot since he appeared to be a straight-laced cop.

I pulled out the chair next to him, then found I couldn't speak. Thick fur covered Knox's face and hands. I recognized his bright amber eyes, but the rest of his face differed from earlier. Knox's features were those of a wolf.

"Yes, Ms. Fontenot, I am a werewolf."

23

———

"**W**ell, um, I-I don't know what to say. You have nice fur."

Knox tapped his fur covered fingers on the table. "It's fine, Ms. Fontenot. Miss Lulu explained you haven't grown up in the magical world for decades."

"I didn't know it existed until a week ago." I forced myself to sit up in my chair, even though it felt like all the experiences and emotions of the last few days were sitting on my shoulders.

"But you grew up here until you were six years old." Knox took a sip of his drink, the ice cubes clinking together in the amber liquid. "So it's true that your mother hid your past from you?"

"Yes, she did. I had no recollection of being a witch or living here, before the ritual today."

"Did you have lapses in memory often before regaining your powers?"

"No. And if you're asking if I forgot killing Chloe, the answer is a definitive no." My whole body grew warm, and I was positive my face was red.

"You do know your police interrogation methods." Knox's tone was serious, but then he laughed. "Ma'am, not every conversation with me is an interrogation."

I said, "Oh." I had never been a suspect, and didn't know how any of this worked in real life.

"Let's chat, as one paranormal to another." Knox waved down a server from across the room. "What would you like to drink?"

"I asked Atlas for a glass of wine." I looked up at the server and did a double take. He appeared human, but he smiled, showing off a set of fangs. I guess I should get used to seeing vampires wherever I go in this town.

"And here it is," Knox said.

I sipped the wine that another server had brought to me. The buttery Chardonnay quenched my thirst and provided a sense of normalcy in this baffling environment. At least wine tasted the same here in this paranormal club.

"I'll take a Sazerac. Would you like to try one, Ms. Fontenot? It's a well-known cocktail here in New Orleans," Knox said.

"I've heard of it, but I don't like whiskey. Are witches supposed to drink whiskey? I've already been told I'm supposed to like tea," I said.

"I'm not that familiar with the requirements of being a witch. I guess it's just one cocktail," Knox said to the server, who walked away instead of turning into a bat as I half expected.

"Do you have a partner, or are you a lone wolf? Oops, sorry, I didn't mean that," I said.

"I think you did," Knox howled.

"You got me." I laughed. His howl was a deep, warm tone, and it didn't frighten me. Granted, if I ran into him in a dark alley, I'd think otherwise.

"Your laugh reminds me of my youngest sister, Cricket." Knox's eyes brightened at her name.

"Cricket? Please don't tell me she's an actual insect." My eyes widened.

"Yes, what's wrong with that?" Knox couldn't keep a straight face. "Sorry, I couldn't help myself. She's a werewolf, too. Cricket is her real name, though."

"Phew, I'm glad I didn't insult you or her then." I breathed a sigh of relief. "Do paranormal abilities run in families?"

"I'm pretty sure they do, except vampires. They're unique."

I casually looked at Atlas behind the bar. Or at least I thought I did.

Knox cleared his throat, and I spun around. I took a sip of my wine, hoping to hide the warmth creeping up my face.

"Atlas is a good man. He's been single as long as I've known him. Every type of paranormal woman has made advances to him, but he's just polite to them." Knox craned his neck to look at Atlas. "He's different around you. You two be careful with each other. Now, that's coming from the big brother in me, not the cop."

"I was going to say thanks, Dad, but I'll refer to you as my big brother instead." I laughed, but inside my emotions bounced all around. I was annoyed that he made assumptions about me and Atlas. But I couldn't deny the sense of warmth that came from his concern. Cricket was lucky to have Knox as a brother.

"My sisters call me their second dad, so it wouldn't have been the first time." Knox grinned. "Let's change the subject. Tell me about yourself. What do you do back in Seattle?"

"I was a buyer for retail stores, but I just quit to go travel with my daughter, Olivia. She's in Australia right now." I felt a lump in my throat after mentioning Olivia. I missed her, and I was worried about how I was going to explain she came from a line of witches. My daughter easily adapted to new situations and people, but finding out your mother had witch powers and she could, too, might just be too much.

"When do you plan to leave?"

"I need to figure out what to do with the family home first. And I assume I'll need to ask you if I can leave." I smiled at the vampire server who placed Knox's drink on the table.

"I should have Miss Chase's murder solved quickly, so hopefully, it will not infringe on your plans."

"What plans?" Evangeline now was by our table. "Hi, y'all. Can I join in?"

"Of course, Miss Evangeline." Knox stood up and pulled out a chair for her. "I was going to ask Miss Lulu about something, but as a longstanding witch, I assume you'll know the answer."

"Are you calling me old?" Evangeline's eyes twinkled.

"Never." Knox smiled.

"You better not." Evangeline laughed. "What's your question?"

Knox took out his notebook from his jacket and flipped a few pages. "Has your coven grown a hybrid plant of jasmine and rose mallow?"

Evangeline turned pale even under the dim lighting. "We call that combination ameliorate. It's forbidden to grow it in all covens."

"I see." Knox scribbled in his notebook and then put it away. He finished his drink in one gulp. "Is this exclusively for witches?"

"Yes. The plant only grows with a complicated spell."

Evangeline took a large sip from my wineglass. She needed the wine more than I did, by the tremor in her voice.

"Miss Fontenot, are you familiar with this plant?"

"No!" I took the wineglass back from Evangeline and downed half of it. "I do not know about this plant, and even if I did, I didn't want Chloe dead."

Evangeline put her arm around me. "Knox, no one in our coven would do this."

"Thank you for the information, Miss Evangeline. I'll be in touch with the coven tomorrow." Knox took his wallet out and placed two twenties on the table. "I'm sorry we couldn't continue our conversation, Miss Fontenot. When the case is over, I hope we can."

Knox left our table and stopped to speak with Atlas, who stood behind the bar. Atlas and I made eye contact, and I expected him to frown or turn away. I assumed Knox told him I was now even more of a suspect in Chloe's murder. If Knox had, Atlas didn't show it. I could feel my cheeks turning red, so I turned back around.

"Oh my, you and Atlas are making googly eyes at each other." Evangeline grinned.

"No, we're not," I said.

"Honey, the attraction between you two is so obvious. We don't date vampires, though, but maybe you'll change that."

"Just out of curiosity, why don't witches date vampires?" I held up my now empty wineglass as the server walked by. Evangeline had finished my drink.

"As you now know, we keep the balance between the living and the dead. Vampires are both living and dead creatures. It makes things complicated when trouble arises with them. Do you keep them away from the dead or away from the living if they're involved in a situation?"

"Have you had to deal with a vampire?" I asked.

"Me, personally? No. Your mom and Lulu worked with Atlas to keep things cordial between the two groups, so nothing has come up in the past fifty years."

"My mom and Luella were close, weren't they?" I said.

"Oh, yes. Not only were they best friends, but your mom insisted Lulu take over the coven when she left town with you. My momma said Lulu was inconsolable for months after y'all were gone." Evangeline grasped my hand. "I was, too. But now you're here! Cheers!"

The server placed our wineglasses on the table and Evangeline raised hers. I did the same, although I felt bad as I hadn't planned to be here forever. But I needed a friend, especially now that I had to figure out the witch skills I had regained. And I needed more information to solve Chloe's death.

"I hate to bring this up, but what can you tell me about the poison that killed Chloe? Is it really only used by witches?" I said.

"Yes, the poison comes from a hybrid plant, ameliorate. Two witches, over a hundred years ago, created the plant. The story goes they expected it to have medicinal qualities, but it turned out to be poisonous." Evangeline stopped talking when the server delivered two plates of crawfish étouffée and a basket of warm French bread with butter.

I sighed at the first bite of the étouffée. The rich gravy was like the gumbo I had earlier, but the focus on this dish was the crawfish. The sweet and salty flavor of the crawfish was subtle, but stood up well next to the spices. The étouffée was on a bed of white rice that soaked up all the good flavors.

"What do you think?" Evangeline asked after we both had eaten half our dinner.

"I loved the gumbo at lunch, but this is fantastic. I'm glad Atlas sent it over."

"Atlas is the most considerate man. I love eating here," Evangeline said.

"He is thoughtful, but let's get back to the poisonous plant." I put down my fork. "I'm going to assume our coven doesn't have this plant."

"We don't! Luella would banish anyone who grew it." Evangeline frowned. "Ameliorate is hard to grow, even for an experienced witch, and then you have to know how to turn it into poison."

"So you don't think a young witch could do it?"

"I doubt it. Oh, you're thinking about Lauren, aren't you?" Evangeline said. "Chloe was mean to her, but I can't imagine sweet little Lauren killing her."

"Me neither." I focused on finishing my crawfish étouf-fée, hoping Evangeline wouldn't see the doubt on my face. I didn't want Lauren to be involved in the murder, but I couldn't count her out.

After finishing my meal, I told Evangeline about my lunch with Lauren. I filled her in on all the information Lauren shared, including Chloe and Trent's interactions and my new knowledge of the Bordelon Coven.

"She told you a ton, didn't she?" Evangeline said.

"Do you think Chloe and Trent could have been up to something with the Bordelon Coven?" I said.

"As much as Chloe could be a pain, I can't imagine her involved with Trent or with the Bordelon Coven." Evangeline shook her head.

"I need to check out this connection. Lauren said they had a tea shop. Can you tell me where it is?"

"I'll go with you tomorrow if you'd like. Can I play Dr. Watson to your Sherlock Holmes?" Evangeline grinned.

"You want to go with me?" I didn't expect Evangeline to offer to help. "I thought you would try to talk me out of going."

"Honey, by the look in your eyes, I know I can't talk you out of going there."

"What's that phrase I keep hearing: Tru dat? Am I using it right?"

Evangeline covered her mouth with her hands, but her laughter spilled out anyway. "See, you're settling back in just fine! Soon you'll be back to saying y'all and I figured."

"I don't know about that, but you are right about the tea shop. Tomorrow I need to go there." I reached over and grasped Evangeline's hand. "If Chloe and Trent were involved with the other coven, it could have something to do with her death."

Evangeline squeezed my hand and then let it go. She waved down our server, three tables away. "Let's head home and get some rest. We have a busy day tomorrow."

"Ladies, can I bring you dessert or a cappuccino?" the server asked.

"No thanks, sugar, we're heading out. We'll take the check," Evangeline said. "It's on me tonight, Thea."

"Atlas took care of your meals, including the tip. If you need anything else, please let me know." The server nodded and left us.

"I'm going out to dinner with you more often if you're getting free meals." Evangeline grinned.

"That was very sweet of Atlas." I mouthed a thank you to Atlas. He smiled and went back to putting liquor bottles on the shelves. Atlas didn't need to buy my meal to keep me coming here. He was enough reason to come back. But I had a murder to solve, and even a handsome man, or rather a vampire, couldn't distract me from my investigation.

24

―――――

Evangeline and I took a cab home from Syncopation and Spirits. It wasn't a long walk to Fontenot Mansion, but my constant yawning concerned her. The driver dropped me off first since Evangeline wanted to make sure I got home safe and sound.

"Thanks for the ride. What time should I be ready in the morning?" I said.

"You're welcome, honey. I'll meet you here at nine and we'll go to Café du Monde." Evangeline closed the door, but then rolled down her window. "Remember not to wear black or all the powdered sugar will show!"

Her laughter trailed off as the cab drove away. Thankfully, I had packed a pair of jeans and a white shirt. I understood what she meant after noticing tourists covered head to toe in white powder.

I opened the gate without using the key. Hearing the lock click open by itself was strange. If I hadn't known I could do it, I would have assumed it was the wine interfering with my senses.

The house was quiet as I entered, which I hoped meant I

could sneak up to my room and go right to bed. No such luck.

"Child, you've been gone all day! I wasn't sure you were coming back home," Luella called out from the living room. I found her sitting on the couch wearing a fuzzy pink robe and holding a teacup.

"You haven't been keeping tabs on me?" I sat across from her on one of the straight-back chairs.

"No, but I will admit I know you talked to your momma." Luella put her cup down on the coffee table. "I spoke with her later. From the way she lashed out at me, I imagine she wasn't happy to see you either."

"No, she wasn't. Let's talk about it tomorrow, Okay? I'm exhausted." I let out an exaggerated yawn.

"We can do that. I could use some rest myself."

I stood up and walked toward the door, but a blast of cold air stopped me. "Wait, is there a ghost here? My mother said the house has ghosts."

"Didn't Fern explain why they're here?" Luella sighed. "No, of course not. As guardians of the living and the dead, we often help those spirits who aren't able to stay in the afterlife. When they become a problem for the living, we offer them sanctuary here."

"Sanctuary? Is this a halfway house for ghosts?" The cold air disappeared as soon as I spoke.

"Now you've insulted her." Luella shook her head. "Hopefully she won't tell all the other spirits."

"How many are here?"

"Let's talk about that tomorrow, too." Luella pushed herself off the couch and that's when I noticed her puffy eyes and red nose.

"Of course. We've both had a long day." I picked up Luella's teacup. "I'll put this in the kitchen for you."

"Thank you, Althea." She brushed her hand on my arm as she passed by me. "You've been through so much today, but I promise things will get easier."

Luella climbed the staircase, the steps creaking until she reached the top. She turned around and gave me a quick smile. I smiled back and went to the kitchen. My eyes grew heavy as I washed the cup and saucer. I agreed with Luella that I had gone through a lot today.

Maybe Luella was right, and things would get easier. But I had my doubts.

25

"Shh! Don't wake her up!"

"It's already seven. I never slept past seven."

I woke up to find two women arguing at the foot of my bed. Technically, they weren't women, but ghosts. They were transparent like my mother was yesterday. The taller one, who claimed she didn't sleep past seven, wore an evening gown with a long train and a tiara. The shorter one wore bellbottoms, a tight T-shirt, and a bunch of Mardi Gras beads.

"It's too late. I'm awake," I said when there was a pause in their conversation. "If you're going to wake me up, you could have at least brought coffee."

"We're ghosts, not your servants, Althea," the woman in the gown snapped.

"Even if we wanted to, we can't hold objects like that. We could push a cup toward you, though." The other woman floated over to my nightstand and pushed a book to the floor.

"Could we not mess up my things? And is there any way

you can stop bringing in cold air with you?" I pulled the covers up to my chin.

"No, we cannot. Stop from being cold, that is." The gowned woman reached out her hand. "My name is Helen Claiborne. Oh, you can't shake my hand. I keep forgetting after all this time."

"I doubt you had a good memory when you were alive, Helen. I'm Destiny Rivers." She sat on the bed. "We used to watch you as a kid."

"Your mother would shoo us away, but we enjoyed watching you learn your magic," Helen said. "We were all sad to see you and Fern leave."

"I'm afraid my mother blocked my memories from our time here, so I apologize for not recognizing you both. Luella said this house was a sanctuary for spirits." I threw the covers off and got out of bed. "Is there a reason you haven't moved on?"

"I hate that word." Destiny frowned. "It sounds like we're hiding from the police."

"We agree on that." Helen floated over to the bookshelf and turned her back to me. "Some of us just aren't ready to go to the afterlife."

"We're here because we caused trouble at our haunting spots." Destiny rolled her eyes. "I only closed the lid on the piano a couple of times at Lafitte's Bar. I couldn't stand listening to that stupid music any longer."

"I'm going to assume Lafitte's is here in the Quarter. Did you die there?" I said.

"I don't want to talk about it." Destiny flipped her hair over her shoulder and disappeared through the bedroom door.

Helen faced me. "Great, now she's going to pout all day.

When Destiny is ready to share her story, she will, but for now, do not ask her."

"Tell her I'm sorry. I'm not familiar with ghost etiquette." I sat back on my bed and rubbed my eyes. This isn't how I planned to wake up after yesterday's chaos.

"That is all right, Althea. I will tell you I'm here because I was disruptive at a restaurant, according to the management." Helen crossed her arms over her chest. "Your family has graciously offered spirits a safe space for generations. I imagine you'll meet most of us soon."

"How many ghosts live here?"

"It varies, but I believe it is ten right now."

"Helen, could you do me a favor?" I said.

Her eyes lit up. "You'd like me to help you?"

"Yes, could you ask all the spirits if they saw anything unusual the night Chloe was killed?"

"Like seeing the murderer?"

"Did you?" My voice went up an octave. Could this be the break I needed?

"Don't blow your wig, Althea!" Helen giggled. "I'm sorry, but no. I saw nothing that night. If anyone else had, they would have mentioned it to Luella."

"Oh." All the energy left my body. "Could you double-check, anyway?"

"I will. Have a wonderful morning!" Helen disappeared through the door.

I flopped back on the bed and closed my eyes. Would I meet any other paranormal beings today? At least Helen and Destiny seemed nice, and Helen offered to help me. But I couldn't wait for information to fall into my lap. Today I needed to find out more about my kind: witches.

Luella had left a note in the kitchen for me. She was out shopping. I couldn't help but wonder if she left so I couldn't question her about my mother and Chloe. We'd have to run into each other at some point in the house, so I went out front to wait for Evangeline.

She was already there, sitting on the top step, next to Tasso.

"There's sleeping beauty! I was going to go with Miss E to get beignets if you didn't come out here," Tasso said.

"You can still come with us. I'll order milk for you or even a café au lait." Evangeline scratched underneath Tasso's chin.

"I appreciate the offer, but all those tourists want to take my photo. Or worse, they try to pick me up since they think I'm a poor little stray thing," Tasso said.

"It must be tough being a magic cat in a non-paranormal place," I said.

"You don't know the half of it, cher." Tasso got up and trotted down to the bottom of the staircase. "You girls have fun, but be careful."

The gate opened on its own and Tasso scampered away.

"Did he open the gate, or did you do that?" I asked.

"Tasso did it. He's got some powers of his own."

"Is he a witch, too?" I followed Evangeline down the stairs and onto the sidewalk.

"He claims he's just a magical cat. How or when he became one is a mystery. He's been around since we were kids, so he must be paranormal, or cats really do have nine lives," Evangeline said.

"I think the fact he talks qualifies him as paranormal." I laughed.

"You're right. I've gotten so used to him, I forget that not all cats talk," Evangeline said.

"Tasso is one of a kind, isn't he?"

"Yes, he is. Now, let's head over to Café du Monde. I'm dying for beignets. It's been ages since I've had them. My stomach always wants them, but my scale says no." Evangeline put her hands on her curvy hips.

"Oh, please, you're perfect and should eat beignets whenever you like. Now, which way do we go?"

26

______

"I'm stuffed. Beignets are addictive."

I brushed powdered sugar off my jeans as Evangeline and I walked out of Café du Monde. While I didn't remember eating beignets as a child, my mouth and stomach did as I scarfed them down. The fluffy, sweet square doughnut like treats needed the strong and bitter café au lait to balance them out.

"They are! We still have so much to talk about, so we'll just come back again." Evangeline's smile was as sweet as the beignets.

We spent the last two hours talking about our lives. I learned Evangeline owned a real estate firm, which explained her flexibility to meet me at all hours. Her daughter, Grace, was a few years older than mine. Grace had the same adventurous nature as Olivia. They were both studying abroad with Grace in Paris and Olivia in Australia.

I learned Evangeline was single, like me, although her story was quite different. I'd never married, but had a few long-term relationships, including Olivia's dad. Evangeline considered herself single because her husband disappeared two years ago.

"You mean he just up and left?" I asked.

"Yes. I'm legally married, but since I haven't heard from Bryce all this time..." Her words trailed off as her lips trembled. When she continued talking, her eyes lost their sparkle. She tried everything, magical and non-magical, to find him. No matter what she did, Bryce's location was a mystery to her and her daughter. I tried to ask more questions about the situation, but Evangeline shot me down.

She plastered on a smile. "No more tales of woe! We have work to do!"

Now we were on our way to the Bordelon Coven shop on Chartres Street. Before we reached the shop, Evangeline stopped to give me advice.

"Now, we are friendly with this coven, but keep your mind blocked. Now that you have your powers, nobody can read your mind unless you allow them. Only a witch in our coven can speak to you telepathically, but don't be surprised if another witch tries to get in your head."

"How do I keep my mind blocked, and why would another witch try to read my thoughts?"

"First, repeat after me. Only my sisters may enter my mind. Anyone else's entry must be declined. For only those whose intentions are pure will keep my soul and mind secure."

I repeated the spell and put my hands on my head as a sharp pain hit me.

"Sorry, I should have warned you it would hurt for a minute. I'm so used to it."

I dropped my hands. "Before I did this spell, could anyone read my mind?"

"No, you need to allow witches from other covens in. But

if you are too relaxed, or the witch is powerful, she could get in."

"There's so much to learn." I took my hands off my head as the pain subsided.

"Don't worry, it'll come back to you!" Evangeline put her arm through mine, and we walked another block until we were in front of Tea, Tarot, and Truth. There was no doubt it was a witch store with a huge witch's hat hanging over the shop door. On either side of the door were two large windows featuring teas in one and crystals in the other.

A bell rang as Evangeline opened the door into the shop. I coughed as the powerful smell of herbs and incense wafted through the air. If I hadn't needed to investigate, I would have left.

"You'll get used to it in a minute," Evangeline whispered.

We were alone in the store, so before a salesperson came out, I studied the shop. As a former retail buyer, I appreciated the organized sections for each type of merchandise. To my right was a wall of shelves filled with jars holding loose-leaf tea, bagged tea, and a variety of tea kettles and cups. Books filled half of the bookcases on the left side wall. Candles, tarot cards, and wands were displayed on the other shelves. A round table held baskets of rocks and crystals. Each one was labeled and included information about its uses. I had no idea turquoise promoted healing and gave protection.

A jewelry case ran the width of the store near the back wall. Behind the case, a small desk held a cash register. Two doors flanked the desk, one marked "Private" and the other, "The Reading Room." As I perused the jewelry case admiring the crystal necklaces, the door labeled "Private" opened. A woman in her early twenties, wearing a long black dress and a witch hat, entered the room. She looked up from her cell phone in her hand and jumped backward, hitting the doorframe.

"Sorry, I didn't realize anyone was here." She shoved her phone in her pocket. "What can I...Oh, you're Fontenot witches."

"We sure are, darling. I don't think we've met. I'm Evangeline." She smiled at the woman.

"I'm Madison." She ripped the witch hat off her head, and a mop of purple curls sprung up. "I only wear the hat for tourists. It's ridiculous, but regular people like the show."

"Oh, yes, the things we do for money." Evangeline laughed. "Are you a newcomer to the city or the shop, Madison?"

"I started working here two months ago. The bayou was boring." Madison turned toward me. "Are you new, too? From the way you're staring at the crystals I guess you're new here."

"You're correct. I'm Althea." I stopped talking when Madison's body stiffened. "Are you okay?"

"Why wouldn't I be?" Madison placed her hands on the jewelry case and gave me a closed-mouth smile. "Are y'all here for something in particular?"

"Yes, we'd love to buy tea. The Bordelon Coven has such a unique variety of blends. Is there anything new for us to try?" Evangeline approached the shelves of teas and pointed at a jar. "I don't think I've tried this Blood Orange Blossom Tea."

Madison's body relaxed as she came out from behind the counter. I stayed by the jewelry case for a few reasons. One, I hate tea and had no interest in it. Two, the crystals in the case fascinated me with their unusual colors. But Evangeline called me over.

"Althea, you've got to smell this tea." Evangeline held the lid of the open jar.

I went over and sniffed the tea and stifled a cough. "It's very fragrant."

"Could we try it? Do y'all still make samples?" Evangeline asked.

"Of course. I'll brew some right now." Madison walked behind the jewelry counter and pulled out an electric teapot. She plugged it in and grabbed a canister and two paper cups from a counter drawer. "What brings you to New Orleans, Althea?" Madison focused on the teapot instead of looking at me.

"I came to take care of my family home. What brought you here?" I laughed, hoping to ease the tension in the room. It didn't work.

"Like I said, the bayou was boring." Madison looked up. "You've had a lot of deaths to deal with, huh?"

"What do you mean?" I played dumb, and Madison took the bait.

"Your coven has had a lot of witches dying lately. I read about Chloe's death. I'm sorry for your loss."

I noted the subtle smirk when Madison said Chloe's name. Evangeline caught it, too.

"Did you know Chloe? Y'all are around the same age," Evangeline said.

"No." Madison poured water into two cups.

"I'm surprised. Chloe liked to go to that bar Dusk, so I thought you'd have met her there." Evangeline picked up a cup and sipped her tea.

I had to stop myself from high-fiving Evangeline. She hit the bull's-eye. Madison's face flushed and her hand quivered as she poured herself a cup of tea.

"We might have crossed paths, but we weren't friends," Madison said.

"I heard Dusk is popular with young witches and vampires. Is that true?" I took a sip of tea and put the cup down. It tasted like a bowl of potpourri.

"Are you looking for clubs to hang out at? Are you a cougar?" Madison's voice was icy.

"Do we look like cougars? Don't answer that!" Evangeline put her cup down as she shook from laughter. "Honey, neither of us are looking for young vampires to date! Men are a pain when they're vampires, too."

"I agree with you, Evangeline." I grinned at Madison, hoping she'd drop her snotty attitude. "Dating is hard enough when you're young, but dating when you're older is so much worse."

"My momma would agree with you. She's looking for husband number three and not having much luck." Madison's shoulders relaxed, along with her tone. "Now, ladies, would you like to buy the tea?"

"Yes, I'll take three ounces," Evangeline said. "How about you, Thea?"

"Oh, I'm good. Can I see one of the crystal necklaces?" I asked.

Madison wrapped up Evangeline's tea and then came over to the case. "Which one do you want to see?"

I pointed at a deep violet crystal hanging on a gold chain. She removed it from the case and handed it to me. It was warm in my hand and sparkled under the lights.

"Wow, it's rare for tanzanite to do that right away." Madison's eyes widened. "You have really strong powers."

Evangeline looked at my hand. "Look at you, Althea! Tanzanite usually takes a few minutes to react to a witch. You could use its powers right now."

Madison snatched the necklace from my hands. "You can't use it unless you buy it. It's two thousand dollars."

"For that price, this crystal should clean my house and make me dinner," I said.

"Witches use it to increase their powers," Evangeline said.

"It's not easy to find, so that's why it's expensive." Madison put the necklace back into the case and locked it.

My whole body went numb and my head throbbed. I rubbed my hands together to get some feeling back into them. Madison stared at me, but didn't say a word. Evangeline pulled me back from the case, and the feeling came back into my whole body. I rubbed the sides of my temples as the headache hadn't left.

Evangeline glared at Madison, who turned her back to us. "How about a turquoise necklace? It's not as expensive."

"No, thanks. I'll just have to save up for the tanzanite," I said. "It's too bad Chloe didn't have this crystal with her when someone poisoned her tea."

I looked at Madison, hoping for a reaction, and it worked.

"Poisoned?" Madison's voice cracked, but she regained her composure. "Who told you that?"

"The detective on her case asked about ameliorate. I've been told that only witches can grow it," I said.

"They banned it decades ago. That's one of the first things I learned when I started my lessons," Madison said.

"Me, too. But if it's true, someone is growing it." Evangeline stepped up to the counter and leaned over. She lowered her voice. "Which coven do you think would break the rules?"

Madison shook her head. "I can't think of anyone. Maybe it wasn't a coven, but another paranormal group."

"But I thought only witches could grow it?" I said.

"There are other people who have similar skills, like the Voodoo priestesses." Madison perked up, like a student who had just realized they knew the answer on a test. "I hope the police go talk to them, especially Priestess Cassandra. She's a sneaky woman; she stole some of our best tarot card clients."

"That's terrible." Evangeline's voice was full of sympathy. "Did she do a spell to steal them?"

"I don't know, but it wouldn't surprise me if she had. If anyone could grow that plant, she could," Madison said.

"Okay, it sounds like we should be careful of Priestess Cassandra's group. I'm sure none of the covens want to lose a member like we lost Chloe," I said.

Time to go, Althea, Evangeline said—inside my head.

"Okay, let's leave," I said, but out loud. I needed to practice talking telepathically. Madison gave me a puzzled look. "Sorry, I just realized I have an appointment in ten minutes. It was a pleasure to meet you, Madison. I haven't met any witches outside my coven."

"But I heard you were at Syncopation and Spirits," Madison said. "You didn't meet any there?"

"Word travels fast around the Quarter! Thank you for the new tea." Evangeline handed Madison money and didn't wait for the change. "Have a blessed day!"

I followed Evangeline to the door, but looked back before leaving. Madison had her phone out and was tapping frantically. I wanted to read her mind, but I didn't need to. Our visit to the store appeared to have agitated her, and she needed to let someone know about it. I just wondered who it was.

27

I tried to talk to Evangeline, but she wanted to wait until we were far away from the shop. We walked up to a path that followed the Mississippi River. We sat at a bench facing the water, and once the group of joggers passed us, Evangeline spoke.

"Sorry to be so pushy, but we have a lot to talk about." Evangeline took a tissue from her purse and blotted her brow.

"We learned a lot, didn't we?" I said.

"Yes, but they learned a lot about you. The way the crystal reacted in your hands definitely worried Madison," Evangeline said.

"Oh, I hadn't thought about that." My years of reading and watching mysteries weren't helping me as I had hoped.

Evangeline patted my hand. "Don't you worry, honey. It was bound to come out that you're a powerful witch. And you're right, we got some information. I don't believe what she said about Priestess Cassandra."

"Does our coven have a good relationship with the Voodoo community?"

"We sure do! They handle any problems with the living and the dead if it relates to Voodoo or anyone in their group."

"Oh, so they're like us in that way. Could they want all the power to control the living and the dead, though?"

"Anything's possible, but I can't imagine they would. We've worked together since Marie Laveau's days," Evangeline said. "Luella hasn't mentioned any problems with them."

"Can we go see this group?"

"Sure, they have a store like the witches. Voodoo Enchantments is over on St. Ann." Evangeline inhaled deeply. "But first, you need to go see your mother again."

"Why?" I crossed my arms.

"Do you remember how you felt after you gave the crystal necklace back to Madison? That was her trying to put a spell on you."

"What?" I uncrossed my arms and stood up.

"Althea, calm down, and let me explain." Evangeline grabbed my hand and pulled me back onto the bench. "She tried to read your mind. Since we did the spell to keep her out of our heads, it didn't work."

"I'm glad it didn't work, but why did I feel so awful? Is that going to happen every time a witch tries to read my mind?" I rubbed my temples, hoping to ward off another headache.

"The reason you were in such pain wasn't from Madison trying to get into your head; she also did a spell to get you to leave."

"All that pain was to get me to leave the shop?" I said.

"No, it was a spell to leave our coven."

"Why would she do that?" I gulped three times, trying to wet my dry throat.

"That's a really good question. You need to talk to Luella. Since she has been acting as leader of our coven, she should talk to Seraphine Bordelon, the head of their coven."

I let out a sigh of relief, as I had no interest in getting involved in witch politics.

"But you need to go to your momma and get all your powers restored." Evangeline's voice was firm, and arguing with her seemed futile.

"Fine. I'll go talk to my mother. Why don't you come with me? She'll probably listen to you more than me." I gave Evangeline my best puppy-dog eyes. "Please."

"As much as I loved your momma, this is between you and her." Evangeline laughed. "Your pleas won't work on me, and anyway, I have to show a house over in the Garden District."

"I need to go to that bar the vampires and witches hang out at and the Voodoo shop," I argued.

"First, see your mother. You shouldn't be around the Bordelon Coven until you can block their spells." Evangeline stood up and offered me her hands. She pulled me up and gave me a hug. "And text me when you're ready to go to the bar and Voodoo shop. Don't go alone."

"You just want to go to the bar to look for young men, don't you?" I laughed.

"Yep, I'm a cougar, all right. Remember, my husband may be missing, but technically I'm still a married woman." Evangeline rolled her eyes. "But seriously, Thea, more trouble is coming to the Quarter. I can feel it in the air."

Evangeline walked to the edge of the river. I walked over to her, sharing the large flat rock that had just enough room for both of us. The brown-tinged water ebbed and flowed close to our feet. We stood shoulder to shoulder. The chatter and footsteps of the people strolling behind us was the white noise I needed to concentrate. If Evangeline was worried, I should be, too. Her witch senses were more attuned to trouble than mine. Of course, I'd been overwhelmed by having my powers restored, talking to my mother, meeting other paranormals, and Chloe's death. Everything that happened to me was trouble as far as I was concerned.

The river breeze brought a peaceful feeling to me. Water always calmed me, whether I was kayaking on the Puget Sound or swimming in the Pacific Ocean. The tourist guidebook I scanned on the plane ride prepared me for the murky color of the water. Sediment made of sand, clay, and silt colored the water on this part of the river, hence the river's nickname, the Muddy Mississippi.

Even though the water wasn't very clear or a pretty blue hue, I still found it comforting. The strong current and the heavy cargo ships heading south showed its strength and purpose. Evangeline shared with me another function of the river.

She opened her purse and took out two lavender bottles. They appeared to be perfume bottles made of a milky glass and were topped with a silver cap decorated with a jasmine motif. Evangeline handed one to me and then she kneeled down. She uncapped the bottle and scooped up the river water. I did the same.

"I guess you're wondering why we're filling bottles with river water." Evangeline grasped my hand and pulled me up with her. "Water from the river or the fountain at Fontenot Mansion is necessary for many spells and rituals. You need to do a protection spell against the Bordelon Coven."

"The entire coven? Not just Madison?"

"Normally I'd say just her since she tried on her own, but she's young. Most witches her age wouldn't attempt a hard spell like that unless instructed by an experienced witch. So..."

"So you think someone told her to get me out of town?" I interjected. Not only had Chloe wanted me gone, but now another coven did, too? Did everyone in the paranormal community want me gone?

"Honey, we just don't know yet." Evangeline hugged me, and for a moment I felt protected and loved.

"When you do a hug, do you put a spell on me to make me feel better?" I wiped my damp eyes as we pulled from our embrace.

"No, darling, it's just me. No magic required." Evangeline's face softened, but there was still concern in her eyes.

"Thanks for being so kind. You're sure you won't come with me to see my mom?"

"My guess is your momma will need to be alone with you, so she'd send me on my way."

"She might send me on my way, too."

"No she won't! Your momma wants the best for you, just like you want the best for Olivia."

I wished I was as confident as Evangeline. My mother and I didn't leave on the best terms at the cemetery the other day. She told me to leave town, but here I was, learning more about my legacy as a witch. Would she refuse to help me gain more of my powers? She might if she believed I'd leave New Orleans if I didn't. My mother was stubborn.

But so was I.

28

———

I had time to prepare myself to see my mother again since the cemetery was on the other side of the French Quarter. Walking through the neighborhood distracted me from my final destination. The color combinations of the cottages and shotgun houses delighted me. The green and yellow pairing was popular, but there were also untraditional mixes like periwinkle and red. The brick townhouses were equally impressive, with elaborate wrought-iron balconies decorated with lush hanging ferns.

Not only was I impressed by the architecture, but I was also taken with the neighborhood's atmosphere. Seattle had never felt this welcoming. From the couple watering their plants on the doorstep to the bicyclist crossing the street by me, everyone said hi. Neighbors chatted with one another from their balconies, and their laughter floated down to the sidewalk. The tour I passed moved to the side at the behest of their guide. Even the tourists smiled or said hi as I reluctantly kept going. I would have loved to stay to hear the history the guide was sharing.

I had never been so mesmerized walking through a city.

While the French Quarter wasn't perfect—I'd never seen so many trashcans full of to-go cups—I felt a connection here that I hadn't expected. Considering I didn't remember my six years living here, I found it strange that I felt somewhat at home. The only thing missing was my daughter.

What was I saying? I shook my head to clear these thoughts out of my head. This wasn't my home. Just because I was now a witch didn't mean I had to stay. Olivia was waiting for me in Australia. Although, after I visited her, I didn't know where I'd go next. Should I consider coming back to New Orleans?

As I reached Rampart Street, the reality of my situation came into focus. If my powers weren't fully returned, staying in New Orleans wouldn't be safe even if I wanted to. There was no point in making plans for the future until my mother returned my powers. Until I could protect myself and take myself off Knox's suspect list, I wasn't going anywhere.

"Althea, you're as stubborn as the afterlife is long," my mother snapped after I called her to me with the spell.

"Very funny, Mom." I rolled my eyes.

"Yes, I'm a laugh riot now that I'm dead." My mother sat on the edge of the tomb and sighed. "Since you're here, I assume Chloe's killer hasn't been found."

"No, but we learned someone poisoned her with ameliorate."

My mother opened her mouth, then shut it. She floated up and paced in front of the tomb. I gave her a moment to collect herself. I learned as a child that it was better to let my mother think quietly than to interrupt her when she was like this. After what seemed like an eternity, but was only thirty seconds, she sat back down on the tomb.

"I imagine they've explained ameliorate to you, so you realize this looks bad for the witch community. And I don't just mean the Fontenot Coven."

"You mean the Bordelon Coven? Evangeline and I visited their shop this morning." I sat next to my mom. "That's the reason I'm here now."

"That coven is as strong as us, or at least they used to be."

"Evangeline said the witch running the store tried to put a spell on me. It was a spell to get me to leave the coven."

"What witch?" My mother's hand reached for mine, but it went through me.

"Her name was Madison. She started working at the shop recently."

My mother's face relaxed. "It wasn't Seraphine Bordelon, then. That's good."

"Why is that good?"

"Seraphine is head of their coven and she is the daughter of my friend Sylvie." My mother's voice faltered when she said Sylvie.

"Is Sylvie the witch who died helping you with the ritual, along with Chloe's grandmother?"

"Yes," she whispered. "I don't want to talk about it now. Please, Althea."

My mother's hands trembled as she grasped the folds of her dress. It was as if she was using every ounce of energy to keep herself in control. If I could have hugged her I would have, but instead I dropped the topic of the ritual.

"Are you were worried that the relationship between the covens disintegrated after you left?"

My mother nodded.

"From what I've been told, everything is fine. Madison could be working on her own," I said.

"You don't believe that. Even as a ghost, I can tell when you're lying." My mother frowned.

"Yes, I'm worried she's part of a bigger problem. Tell me what you know about the other coven members who passed away before you. Luella says that someone killed them, including you. What do you..."

I stopped talking as a tour guide with twelve people turned down the row. The guide came by me and ushered his group ahead of him. "Friends, let's keep going so we can give this woman some peace and quiet. As I said, this is a real cemetery, not a movie set."

Some of the group avoided looking at me while others stared at me as if I were part of the tour. One woman said, "I'm sorry for your loss." Another elbowed her husband when he said, "How much is a tomb worth?"

Once the group was at the end of the aisle, the tour guide turned to me and took off his Panama hat. "Miss Fern, I hope the afterlife is treating you well. It's good to see your daughter is here now."

"Thank you, Elijah. My best to you and your family," my mother said. "I haven't seen your sister yet, but I'll keep an eye out for her."

"I'd appreciate that." Elijah put his hat back on. "Sorry I have to run, but if you need anything, Miss Althea, your momma has my information."

"Thanks," I said before Elijah joined his tour group.

"Only those with spiritual powers can see ghosts. Elijah is a psychic and used to frequent the coven's shop. He liked my grandmother's cornbread." My mother gave a slight smile.

"Who is Elijah's sister? Was she in the coven?"

"She passed away decades ago, but no, she wasn't a witch." My mother stood back up and stretched her arms over her head. "Let's get back to why you're here. Did Luella send you to get more powers?"

"Actually, it was Evangeline who insisted I needed more of my powers to protect myself. I know you don't want me involved in the witch world, but I have no choice while I'm in New Orleans."

My mother paced once again, her ghostly image fluttering with each turn she made. The sky darkened when my mother finally stopped in front of me. "I am not happy about this, but it appears there is no other way to keep you safe."

"Thank you." I relaxed my hands; I hadn't realized how hard I was gripping them.

Fern nodded and inhaled deeply. "This will feel strange, but you must sit still."

Before I could agree, my mother floated through me. My body shivered, and the pain in my head was worse than any migraine I'd experienced. I squeezed my eyes shut and gritted my teeth as my mother went back and forth through me nine times.

"There. It's done," Fern whispered.

I blinked my eyes to acclimate to the bright sunshine that replaced the clouds. My body wasn't shivering, but there was a strange sensation running from my head to my toes. It was as if my body was surging with energy.

"You'll feel strange as your powers settle into you, but you'll be fine."

"Thanks, Mom." My legs wobbled as I stood up and my mother tried to steady me, but her hands went through me. We both laughed at the awkwardness of the situation. I missed her laugh and wished I could hear her do it more often.

"Is there anything I should know or do now?

"Study your spellbook and practice the protections spells with Luella. She's the best teacher in the coven."

"I will." I took in a deep breath, knowing this next conversation wouldn't be pleasant. "Mom, Luella believes you were murdered along with three other witches: Donna, Betty, and Chloe."

"Me? It was a hit-and-run, I thought."

"That's what I said, but then I thought about it a little more. It was broad daylight and I can't see how the person didn't know you were there," I said gently. Suggesting to your mother that she had been murdered was a delicate conversation. Or at least I thought.

"That makes complete sense now! Every car that ever came by me when I got my mail always saw me!" She balled her hands up. "What did the police say?"

"At first, I agreed with them it was a hit-and-run."

"And they hit me hard, so the car must have been speeding very fast."

I squeezed my eyes shut at the image of my mother laying on the street. She looked like a discarded rag doll. The police wouldn't let me get close enough to see her injuries, but I didn't need to. I screamed and collapsed on the ground, knowing my mother was dead.

"There were no skid marks on the road. The police assumed it was a drunk driver," I said.

"It could have been, but tell me about these other deaths and why Luella thinks it's happening. I didn't listen to Lulu when she insisted Donna and Betty were murdered."

I relayed the information Luella gave me to my mother,

who listened quietly. Once I finished, my mother sat next to me.

"Althea, I'll ask Donna and Betty what they remember about their deaths. Chloe has been hiding, but I'll find her."

"Can't you call them here now?" I sighed.

"No, I can't just snap my fingers. Unless you have their ashes or their dead bodies, you can't summon them."

My stomach dropped. "Hold it. If I didn't have your ashes, I would need your body to call you? What kind of weird ritual is this?"

Fern's laughter lit up her face. "You are so serious, Thea! If I was buried, you would just need to come to the tomb and do the ritual. You can have my ashes put in the tomb if you like."

"No, I enjoy carrying around your ashes in my purse. It's completely normal." I giggled with my mom. Go figure we'd have a lighthearted bonding moment in a cemetery with her as a spirit and me as a witch.

Fern stopped laughing. "Let's get back to the issues at hand. I'll go find the witches and see what they remember."

"Can you get them here now?"

"They might be busy, Althea. Just because we're dead doesn't mean we're, well, dead." My mother winked. "There's a lot of fun here in the afterlife if you're looking for it."

I hadn't realized how much I missed my mother's dry sense of humor. She had a serious nature, but I loved when she joked or laughed. "Okay, Miss Party Animal, I'll come by tomorrow and see if you've found them. But let me ask another question. Could anyone in the Voodoo community have had anything to do with these murders?"

"Never say never, but we've always had a good relationship with Priestess Casandra's temple. Voodoo is largely a matriarchal community, so we have that in common."

"Voodoo is always evil in movies, though."

"Tsk tsk, don't believe any of that mumbo jumbo. Voodoo, like any religion, can be distorted for evil purposes. Our coven has more in common with them than other paranormal groups."

I twirled my hair, now more confused than before. "The Bordelon witch mentioned them, so you don't think they could grow the poisonous plant or want to take over our powers?"

"Again, never say never, but I doubt it's them. But you can talk to Priestess Casandra at her shop, Voodoo Enchantments. Please be respectful."

"Of course I will. Anyone else I should look into?" I said.

"I said just talk to her, not investigate her. Althea Rose, don't get yourself into trouble. Let the police handle it. Who's the detective investigating Chloe's death?"

I ignored her command not to investigate because that's what I was going to do, no matter what she said. "Knox Dupriest is on the case. He considers me a suspect."

"Knox is a good man and he'll clear you soon. Do you know he's a—"

"Werewolf? Yes, I discovered that at Syncopation and Spirits."

"The place is still open?"

"Yes, and Atlas says hi."

"You've met Atlas? He's back in New Orleans?"

"Yes, he was shocked it had been thirty years since he'd seen you last."

"Vampires lose all sense of time." My mother gave me one of her rare smiles that lit her face. The joy of seeing her happy turned to sadness as I remembered that I'd never see her smile in real life again.

"That's what he said."

"Atlas's club was so elegant."

"That describes him, too." As soon as the words slipped out of my mouth, my face felt like it was on fire.

"Didn't Luella warn you not to get involved with vampires?" My mother frowned.

"She did, but may I remind you that at my age, I'm very selective of the men I date. Vampires are not on the list." I laughed, hoping it sounded authentic.

"Good. Don't go messing with vampires or any other magic people. It's just too complicated."

"Is that why you took us away from here? Did you and my father have problems? Was he a vampire? Please don't tell me it's Atlas." I shuddered.

"Atlas is not your father, but I don't want to talk about your father right now."

I frowned, and then I tried to remember my childhood. Nothing came up. My mother must not have given me back the power to remember my childhood. I could tell from my mother's stern expression that she wouldn't return my memories tonight. I'd let it go for now, as much as I wanted to demand she tell me about my past. One thing at a time, for now.

Another idea came to me, though. "Mom, I met two of the ghosts in the house, Helen and Destiny. They said they watched me as a child."

"They're still there? They should have moved on by now. Then again, they did like hanging out with you and Evangeline when you were kids."

"Could you stay at the mansion? If you wanted to, that is."

"I could, but I have work to do in the afterlife." My mother looked away from me.

"What work?" I stood up and walked in front of my mother.

"Now's not the time to talk about it." Fern crossed her arms. "You need to go to Lulu and practice your new powers."

I gave an internal scream, but my frustration must have shown on my face.

"Listen, I'm not going anywhere. We can talk about other things, but for now, let's get your name cleared. And you need to make sure you and the rest of the coven are safe." My mother lowered her voice to a whisper. "You need to be careful, Thea. If Luella is right, there is a witch killer out there."

29

"The girl did what?" Luella whipped her head around to face me in the kitchen. "This is not good, not good at all."

I left the cemetery after lying to my mother that I would just go by the Voodoo shop to chat, not investigate. I also promised not to look into the Bordelon Coven on my own. That was another lie. While my mother had the utmost faith in Knox, she wasn't the one on his list of suspects. But I kept my promise to talk to Luella.

The scent of bananas lured me to the kitchen, where I found Luella at the stove, stirring a pot of banana pudding. I loved any kind of pudding, but especially banana.

"Don't burn the pudding!" The smell of scorched bananas filled the air. I moved the pot off the burner. "I'm sorry. I should have waited until you were finished cooking."

"No, it's my fault. I'll make another batch. Can't let these vanilla wafers go to waste." Luella took another pot out, but didn't start cooking. "Tell me everything. Leave nothing out."

Luella didn't interrupt me as I shared what happened at

the tea shop and with my mother at the cemetery. Luella was stone-faced as she listened, which ratcheted up my anxiety. This news couldn't be good.

"Well, Thea, you're one busy witch."

Luella opened a cabinet and took out a bottle of bourbon and two glasses. She poured a measure into each cup. I sat down with her at the table and accepted the glass. While I took a sip, Luella drank hers in one gulp.

"You're worried about the Bordelon Coven, aren't you?" I said.

"I hope that young witch was just trying out her powers, but we must be careful."

"Yes, that's why Evangeline insisted I get my mother to reinstate all my powers."

Luella nodded and refilled her glass. This time, she sipped it. "Evangeline is a smart cookie. I'm glad to hear your momma listened to reason."

"At least when it came to my powers." I shuddered after I finished the rest of my bourbon all at once. "She didn't give me my memories back."

"No point in worrying about that." Luella pushed her chair back from the table. "Let's go practice those protection spells now. I have a meeting with the Lambert Coven in Algiers Point to see if they have had any trouble like ours."

Luella slowly rose from her chair and put the pot of burned pudding in the sink. "I'll clean this up later. Let's go out to the fountain. You'll need to carry water with you for some of these spells."

I took out my bottle of river water. "Evangeline and I got river water this afternoon. Do I need water from the fountain, too?"

"Nope, that'll work. Let's go do some magic."

"Ancestors, I call on your shield of protection. Gaze into my heart and find my pure reflection. I wish no harm to a fellow witch in any direction, just safety for my coven and those with a shared connection."

I dropped a handful of jasmine flowers into the water fountain. Five times in a row, they vanished in smoke when hitting the water. A surge of heat started at my feet and exited from the top of my head.

I wiped the sweat off my brow. My breathing and heart rate returned to normal after being fast-paced each time I recited the incantation. "This is a better workout than spin class."

"It'll get easier as you go, but this spell will always wear you out. Be sure to drink some water afterward. Not your protection water, though."

"I have no desire to drink anything from the Mississippi River." I followed Luella back up to the kitchen. Taking two bottles of water from the fridge, I gave one to her.

"Thank you. Although you're more prepared, don't relax. Be on guard now that everyone knows you're here." Luella drummed her fingers on the kitchen table. "This spell will protect you for seven days, so we'll repeat it next week. But maybe I should stay home with you. Or you could come with me to Algiers."

I blocked my mind before I answered. "No, thanks. I'm tired and want to rest for a bit."

Luella's eyes bore into me. "You're not going to get into trouble now, are you?"

"I don't plan on it." Now that was true. I didn't want to get into trouble. But I wouldn't sit around twiddling my thumbs.

"I hope you're not lying. You've learned to block your mind, I see." Luella gave a tight-lipped smile. "Don't confront anyone in the Bordelon Coven, all right? We want to keep on civil terms with them."

"Unless they had something to do with Chloe's death," I said.

"Of course. I pray no witches are involved." Luella put her hand on my arm. "But if they are, they will pay for what they've done."

30

Luella left thirty minutes later, after I promised I would be fine on my own. As soon as I closed the door after her, the ghosts appeared.

"You're going out, aren't you, Thea?" Destiny sat on the stairs, grinning.

"We heard what Luella said to you. Thea, don't go getting into trouble." Helen floated around me, her ball gown swishing around her.

"I'm going to take a walk around the neighborhood." I tried to walk around Helen, but she stopped in front of me. "It's a gorgeous night. In Seattle, all we have is rain this time of year."

"Sure. We believe you." Destiny giggled. "It's just like the time I told my parents I was going to the movies when I ended up at Woodstock."

"Oh, no, you're not telling that story about that distasteful event?" Helen wrinkled her nose. "You better leave now, or you'll be stuck hearing about Destiny sleeping in mud and her supposed dalliances with musicians."

"It wasn't distasteful, and my dalliances were not

supposed." Destiny huffed. "But yes, if you're going out, you better go now before Luella puts a spell to keep you here."

"What?" My stomach clenched. "Can she do that to me?"

"I was just kidding." Destiny floated next to me and pointed to the front door. "But you never know what Luella can do. I've been here for over fifty years and she still surprises me."

"Be careful, Althea!" Helen called after me as I left the house. When I got back tonight, I planned to read through my spellbook. I needed to be prepared to use all my powers if necessary.

Why didn't I look in my grimoire before I got here?

I was outside the Dusk bar, figuring out how to go inside without being caught. As I watched twenty something men and women go inside, I knew I'd stand out like a sore thumb.

I leaned up against a street light and opened my purse. There wasn't enough light to read my spellbook. I wouldn't go unnoticed even if I tried. A middle-aged woman reading a leather-bound book by a gaslight at 8:00 p.m. would draw attention.

Just as I came to my senses that I'd need to find a quiet, non-paranormal place to read my book, a person's arrival surprised me. Lauren, dressed in a short, pink skirt and a matching low-cut blouse, stumbled toward the bar in her black stiletto heels. She looked uncomfortable as she pulled down the skirt and clutched her purse tightly to her side. Even from a distance, I saw her fake eyelashes that fluttered like moths trapped in a bug zapper.

Why was Lauren here? Besides looking unsure of her

outfit, she also appeared nervous from the way she was biting her lips. If she were involved with the Bordelon Coven or with Trent, my heart might break. At lunch, she was so kind and seemed so dedicated to our coven. Could she be looking into Chloe's visits to the bar? Or worse, was she trying to take Chloe's place?

As I was contemplating confronting her, Madison walked out and approached Lauren. I tried to read their minds, but they either had them blocked, or I was too far away.

All I could go by was their interaction. While they didn't hug each other, their faces appeared relaxed and they smiled. If Madison hadn't tried to hex me earlier, I would have been happy to see Lauren being social and happy.

If I couldn't hear them, I was just going to have to go over to them. At least I could try to read their reactions when they saw me. They shouldn't object to talking with me if this was a friendly meetup. If they were up to something, my presence would cause a stir.

Trent's arrival stopped me in my tracks. Apparently vampires didn't change their clothes like ghosts, since Trent wore the same James Dean outfit as before. His slicked-back hair glistened in the light over the bar's door. He put his arm around Lauren who immediately shrugged it off. At least that was a good sign. She gave him a dirty look and then spoke to Madison briefly. Lauren entered the bar on her own.

After the door closed, Madison dragged Trent to the other side of the bar door. They were closer to me, but I still couldn't hear them. Fortunately, their body language gave me a bit of a picture. Madison spoke with her arms, poking at Trent's chest and putting her hands on her hips. Trent smirked as she talked, but stopped when she grabbed for the chain attached to his jeans pocket.

Madison winced as Trent held on to her wrist. Whatever hung from his chain, Trent didn't want to show it to her. Now I wanted to see it, too, but I didn't think Trent would be so accommodating.

Trent released her wrist and stuck his hand in his other pocket and pulled out a crystal on a chain. I recognized the stone as the type Madison showed me at the shop. But this tanzanite crystal was larger and hung on a thick gold chain. The one at the shop cost two thousand dollars, so this one must be worth at least twice or triple the price.

Madison stopped rubbing her wrist and accepted the necklace from Trent. She dropped it into her purse and took out an envelope. Was she paying him for the necklace? *Open the envelope, Trent!* I screamed in my head, hoping it would make him do it.

It did not.

Trent gave her a toothy smile and slipped the envelope inside his coat. Madison whispered in his ear and then entered the bar. I expected Trent to go inside, too, but he didn't. He looked around the area, and I got what felt like a lump in my throat, assuming he saw me. If he had, he didn't yell or come toward me. He took three steps and turned into a bat. He flew in the opposite direction and once again flew into a gaslight. I held back a laugh as he flew haphazardly through the air before straightening out and disappearing into the night.

My amusement disappeared as quickly as Trent. I needed to know what the deal was between him and Madison. It might have nothing to do with Chloe's murder, but my intuition said otherwise. I could go inside and confront Madison, but I decided to learn more about Trent.

There was one place and one person who had information about Trent. Time to go to Syncopation and Spirits and talk to Atlas.

31

My stomach churned with nerves, not hunger. Evangeline would say I was antsy because I was looking for Atlas. Yes, I needed to find Atlas, but for information, not romance. My intuition said the necklace and envelope exchange between Trent and Madison was more than a simple transaction. Without proof, I had to avoid accusing them of illegal activities. But I wouldn't ignore my gut.

This time, they welcomed me with smiles instead of stares when I entered the room. The same group of fairies were in the back corner, laughing and sipping their drinks. They either improved their behavior or it was just an early hour. Around a large table, next to the fairies, pale men and women drank what looked like red wine. I didn't want to know if it was wine or blood, so I hurried to an empty table at the side of the stage.

I hadn't even scooted forward in my chair when a server stood by my elbow. "Good evening, Miss Fontenot. What can I get you to drink?"

"You know my name?"

The server's fangs sparkled in the dim light as she smiled. "The French Quarter is a tight-knit community, especially among the paranormals. A new witch in town sparks all kinds of talk."

"I should have guessed. Hopefully, it's good information going around." I twisted a lock of my hair.

Before the server answered, a woman took the chair next to me. "Of course it's all good. We're so happy to have a Fontenot witch back in our midst." She turned to the server. "I'll have a Sazerac. Althea, what would you like?"

"A Chardonnay, please."

The server nodded and walked away without another word. I directed my attention to the woman at my table. "I'm sorry, but who are you?"

"My name is Seraphine Bordelon." Seraphine's deep-blue eyes flashed annoyance while her glossy pink lips formed a smile. "Miss Luella hasn't spoken of me?"

"Luella is busy dealing with the loss of one of our coven's members," I said, trying to keep the irritation out of my voice. I knew who she was, but I would not give her the satisfaction of telling her.

"Of course she has. Forgive my manners." Seraphine stuck out her hand. "Let me start again. Hello, I'm Seraphine, head of the Bordelon Coven."

"Althea Fontenot." I shook her hand, noting the gold signet ring with a flower embossed on the top. "That's a beautiful ring."

"Thank you. It's our coven's ring. The flower is Camellia sinensis." She tapped the top of the ring with her a long, glossy red nail.

"That makes sense, since your coven is known for its tea."

"Madison told me you and Evangeline came by our shop today."

"News travels fast in the French Quarter."

"It does. I wish I had been there to welcome you. We need to get together as coven leaders to discuss the state of witchcraft here," Seraphine said.

"I'm not in charge of the Fontenot Coven. Luella is."

Seraphine gave a little gasp. "But Luella isn't a Fontenot! She's done an adequate job in your mother's absence, but since you're here now, she should step down."

"I'll make a note of your concern." This woman was a piece of work. I couldn't imagine questioning the leadership of another coven, especially to someone who had just returned.

"Oh my, I didn't mean to overstep my bounds. Please forgive me." Seraphine sounded sincere, but once again, I saw that flash of annoyance from earlier.

"You're very passionate about the community." I paused as Seraphine nodded. "I only recently learned about my heritage, so Luella is the best woman to lead the coven."

"So it's true? You don't remember your childhood here? We used to play as children since our mothers were friends." She smiled at me.

Apparently, I played with all the witch children. The server arrived with our drinks and left without asking if we wanted to order food. Before I could call her back, Seraphine said, "It was difficult for me when you left, especially since my mother had just died in a ritual your mother led."

I choked on my wine and raised my napkin to my mouth. The napkin wasn't big enough to cover my face entirely, but I wished it were. This wasn't new information, but I guess I didn't expect her to be so blunt. But then again, if my mother had died in a ritual her mother performed, I would be blunt, too.

"I'm making a mess of this, aren't I?" Seraphine handed me another napkin. "Did I surprise you with that news?"

I dabbed my lips with the napkin and cleared my throat. "No. I know about it, but not in detail. I'm sorry for your loss."

"Thank you." She finished her cocktail. "I don't know the details of the ritual either. Your mother apologized to everyone before disappearing with you. I saw her on her yearly visits, but she was never willing to talk about my mother's death."

"My mother never talked about it with me either. I'm sorry I don't have any information for you."

"Have you spoken to your mother since she passed away? Your coven can speak to those beyond the veil."

"Yes, so I've been told. I believe someone has tried to reach out to Chloe." I wanted to switch the conversation from my mother to Chloe. Fortunately, Seraphine went along with it.

"Yes, poor Chloe. It's a shame when one of our own dies so young." Seraphine traced the rim of her glass with a finger, and her glass magically was refilled. "Have the police identified a suspect?"

"Not that I've heard," I lied. There was no reason to share I was a suspect. "Do you have any theories since you're familiar with everyone in the paranormal society?"

Seraphine pulled her shoulders back. "I am a leader in the community. The local covens are on good terms. But there are other groups that aren't on the same page as us."

I leaned over the table. "Who are they?"

"I'm not one to gossip." Seraphine looked around the room and then scooted closer to me. "But you should know whom to be wary of. There are many members of the local Voodoo temples that don't like witches. They say we're weaker versions of them."

"Thanks for telling me." I appreciated her information, but until I vetted it myself, I wouldn't trust it. "How about vampires? Do they get along with us?"

"We don't have any issues with vampires. They're all wonderful."

Obviously, she had no problems with Trent like I had. Or she might have lied. Her voice sounded sincere, but I noticed her mouth twitch when she said "all."

"Would you like another drink?" I waved to our server, who nodded at me. Maybe he'd bring me a second drink without asking.

"No, thank you. I need to drive back home to the bayou." Seraphine opened her purse and took out her wallet. "Let me give you my card. We should get together."

"The drinks are on the house, Seraphine." Atlas stood next to our table. "Good evening, ladies."

"You're too kind, Atlas. It's good to see you." Seraphine floated from her chair and sauntered up to Atlas. He furrowed his brows as she kissed him on the cheek.

If I were interested in Atlas, I would be jealous of Seraphine's familiarity with him. Her hand rested on his arm as she beamed at him.

If I were interested in Atlas, his warm smile would have made me jealous.

But I wasn't interested in Atlas, so it didn't matter. At least that's what I told myself.

"It's good to see you, too, Seraphine. I'm happy to see you've met Thea." Atlas slipped his hand from underneath Seraphine's hand. His fangless smile toward me almost made me forget my momentary jealousy—jealousy I would have had if I were attracted to Atlas.

"Yes, Seraphine introduced herself. She was just giving me her card before she left." I extended my upturned hand, waiting for Seraphine to drop her card in my palm.

She rummaged in her purse and pulled out her card, which only had her name and phone number on it. She didn't drop it in my palm, but put it on the table. "Call me so we can chat about our mutual business. We'll talk soon."

Seraphine turned back after taking a step. "Atlas, we should catch up, too. I found a copy of the album *Ella and Louis* that I'm sure you'd love to listen to."

"Thank you for thinking of me." Atlas's voice was polite but noncommittal.

Seraphine gave a quick wave as she navigated through the tables in her stilettos. All eyes were on her as she left the club, and once she was gone, the chatter of the patrons and clinking of glasses and silverware returned.

"I take it this was your first time meeting Seraphine?" Atlas sat in her former chair.

"How did you guess?"

"Everyone has the same reaction to meeting her—a bit of awe mixed with annoyance." Atlas laughed.

"I am not in awe of her," I snapped. "Seraphine is a confident woman. I'll give her that. You and she seem friendly."

"As the club's owner and member of the vampire council, I build good relationships with other leaders in the paranormal community."

"So you're friendly to all the head witches?"

"I am, but that's not what you're really asking, is it?" Atlas winked. "No, I'm not going steady with Seraphine. Is that even the right phrase this decade?"

"Dating is a better phrase. But then again, I'm a frumpy old lady." I hoped my tone was light, as I didn't want to get into a serious conversation about dating. I had other things I needed to address. But Atlas didn't let me get away with my self-deprecating remark.

"Thea, you are anything but frumpy and old. Me, on the other hand..."

"Okay, let's agree we're both not old or frumpy." I laughed. "So tell me, what's the vampire council? What do you do?"

Atlas blew out his cheeks. "It's not very exciting. We keep our existence as quiet as we can. Vampires want to live alongside humans and other paranormal creatures in harmony. When someone threatens that balance, we work with them."

"Trent must go in front of the council often." I turned to the server, who stood next to me with a tray. "That's not mine. I didn't order food yet."

"I took the liberty of having a meal brought out for you. Hopefully, you like fried green tomatoes with shrimp. If not, we'll get you something else," Atlas said.

"This looks wonderful, thank you."

"To confirm your earlier statement, Trent has come before the council many times. It's never been for anything truly malicious, just overindulging in our ways."

I put my fork down, mid-bite. "Does that mean he's bitten too many people? Or drank all their blood?"

"I'm sorry. I shouldn't have said this while you're eating. But no, Trent has drained none of his donors, for lack of a better word. He enjoys interacting with humans and occasionally taking their personal possessions along with their blood." Atlas grimaced as he spoke.

"His attack on me was just an everyday thing for him?" I shook my head.

"No, it's not an everyday thing, as you say, but he has mugged tourists for their jewelry. We try to return it to them when we catch him."

"Does Trent need money that badly?" The exchange between him and Madison could have just been a financial arrangement. Assuming the envelope contained cash. But as I stared at my empty glass, the more I believed Madison gave Trent poisoned tea. My concern must have showed on my face.

"Thea, has Trent bothered you again? If he's tried to rob you, you need to let me know." Atlas's hand covered mine. It was warm to the touch.

I shook my head. "No, I'm just curious about the paranormals I've met so far."

"Tell me if he causes trouble again. I don't want Trent to sully your impression of me." Atlas blushed and pulled his hand away. "I mean vampires."

"Oh, I knew what you meant." His embarrassment made him even more charming, but I pushed my feelings aside. "Seraphine says witches and vampires are allies, but not with the Voodoo community. Do you know why?"

"No, I haven't heard of any problems."

"Interesting. I'd like to meet Priestess Cassandra. Is the shop open now?" I took out my cell phone to look up the location.

"Althea, take another witch with you when you go."

I looked up from my phone at Atlas. "Your face is so serious. What's wrong with Priestess Cassandra?"

"I'm sorry. I didn't mean to cause concern. It's just that you haven't been around Voodoo since you were a child," Atlas said.

"What does that mean?"

"Voodoo is a powerful religion, like your witchcraft. You should go with someone so you're not overwhelmed."

"Why don't you come with me, then?" I said.

"I can't."

"Or won't?" My voice didn't hide my impatience. "Just spill it. Why are you afraid of Voodoo?"

Atlas gritted his teeth. "I'm not afraid of them. My experiences with the community were problematic. Don't accept their promises at face value."

I tried to read Atlas's mind, but I couldn't. It was probably just as well. If I started prying into the minds of my friends, I might learn information without context. Or worse—information about me I might not want to hear. But I didn't need to read his mind to understand that he had serious concerns about me going by myself to the Voodoo shop.

"Hopefully, one day you'll tell me about your experience. I'll take your advice and take Evangeline with me tomorrow," I said.

"Thank you." The muscles in his face relaxed. "How do you like the dish?" Atlas asked.

"It's amazing." I patted my stomach. "So, is it true vampires can't eat or drink? Besides blood, I mean."

"It's true. Nothing for us. I miss a good slice of pecan pie with whipped cream."

"So no tea? Or wine?" I added the last question so he wouldn't connect my question to the Bordelon Coven. I kept my concerns about the coven to myself.

"No, food or drinks make us ill. We're good at pretending to eat or drink, so please invite me to any dinner parties you host," Atlas laughed.

"Well, my cooking is nothing to write home about, so

you're not missing out." I wasn't lying. My cooking was pretty basic, like grilled cheese sandwiches and boxed pasta with jarred sauce. The food in New Orleans was unlike anything I've made before.

I loved the food here, but I didn't like the tea. Especially the tea from the Bordelon Coven's shop. Now that I knew vampires drank nothing, I doubted Madison had given Trent a bag of tea for his personal use. But I needed more information before I went to the police with my theory. Knox struck me as the kind of detective who wanted every i dotted and every t crossed before he arrested anyone.

Tomorrow I needed to find out more about Madison and Trent. But I needed to meet Priestess Cassandra first. The more paranormals I met might lead me to the truth.

32

"Here we are. This is the Voodoo shop," Evangeline said.

"No, this isn't ominous at all," I said.

"Well, it's a good thing you waited for me to come here, unlike last night." Evangeline wagged a finger in front of me like I was a naughty schoolgirl.

In a way, I was. I called her this morning and filled her in on last night. My visit to Dusk by myself upset Evangeline, especially when I told her about Madison, Lauren, and Trent's interactions. She breathed a sigh of relief when I said I didn't go into the bar. We met this morning at Café du Monde and beignets smoothed everything over.

Now we stood in front of Voodoo Enchantments. If it wasn't for the sign over the door, I would have assumed this was a run-down cottage. Green paint barely covered the wood siding, and faded black shutters flanked the entrance to the store. Although it was almost noon, the interior of the shop was dark.

"Oh, there's nothing to worry about. Trust me."

I followed Evangeline up two chipped cement steps to

enter the shop. A bell rang through the shop as the door opened and closed. The dim lighting didn't keep me from seeing the strangest selection of merchandise. The right wall was decorated with Voodoo dolls in various shapes and sizes. Some were made of brightly colored fabric with cheerful faces. Others were made in gray or black fabric with X-s for the eyes and mouths. I would have turned right around if I didn't have a reason to go inside.

Around the rest of the room were shelves with books, candles, bottles with labels like "love potion" and "brick dust," and packets of herbs. At first, I was a bit spooked by the small coffin-shaped box that said it was a "Voodoo Ritual Kit." The directions on the box said the doll, paper, incense, and oil were all you needed to do your own ritual. But then I remembered I had done a ritual with jasmine flowers and river water, and what was the difference?

The wood planks creaked as I shuffled farther into the store toward a polished, wood table with an antique cash register and an extensive selection of tarot cards. There was a plaque explaining that a variety of psychic readings were available, including tarot cards, palms, and bones. Okay, now whose bones did they read?

Before I could ask Evangeline, the fabric curtain behind the sales counter was pushed aside by the most elegant woman I had ever seen. Dressed in a maxi-dress of shimmering purple, she wore a matching scarf on her head. Her posture accentuated her height of at least five feet ten inches. Gold necklaces dripped down to her slender waist.

"Good day, Priestess Althea. I am happy to make your acquaintance. I am Priestess Cassandra." She came from behind the sales counter and offered me her hand.

"It's just Althea." I accepted her firm handshake. "I'd say

I was surprised you know my name, but everyone seems to know everyone in this town."

Cassandra's warm laugh relaxed me, which was impressive, considering how unnerved I felt when I entered the shop. I repeated the blocking ritual in my head in case Cassandra could read minds, too.

"That is true, especially in our special community." Cassandra turned to Evangeline, who was sorting through a basket of bundles of what looked like strips of white paper. "Let me know if you're looking for something particular, Evangeline."

"Thank you kindly, Priestess Cassandra. Do you have the bundles of sage and lavender?" Evangeline said.

"I do. I have a new shipment of them in the back room. Let me close the shop, and I'll take you to my private area." Cassandra locked the shop door and then gestured for us to follow her through the curtain behind the sales counter.

The room was a combination library, storeroom, and tiny kitchen. To the left was a seating area with four red-velvet wingback chairs and two round side tables. Two bookshelves stood behind the area.

To the right were shelves of boxes of the shop's inventory and supplies. A few potted plants were interspersed between the boxes. Along the back wall was a sink, and one cabinet with shelves above, holding glass jars of coffee and tea. A small refrigerator sat in between the cabinet and a long console table.

"This is beautiful back here. It doesn't seem like a store at all," I said.

"Thank you. The front of the shop is for the tourists. No real practitioner is going to buy a Voodoo doll. We make our own," Cassandra said. "Back here is for my friends and family. That's my altar there. Feel free to go look."

Cassandra pointed to the table in the back of the room. I took her up on her offer and inspected her table. A drawing of Marie Laveau took centerstage on her altar. Tasso had told me about her, so I didn't have to ask. Surrounding the portrait were a hairbrush, a mini bottle of rum, and green bead necklaces. Two white candles and two blue candles burned next to a human skull. Was this the bones that Cassandra used for her psychic readings? Or was the service BYOB—bring your own bones?

"I just made a pot of coffee or would you prefer tea?" Cassandra held a French press maker in her hand.

"Coffee for me, please." The powerful aroma of chicory coffee was too good to pass up.

"A witch that prefers coffee? I like you already." Cassandra laughed. "No offense, Evangeline."

"None taken. I like coffee, but if you have any of your peppermint tea, I'd love it," Evangeline said.

"Let me get the kettle on. Now, tell me, Priestess Althea. Sorry, Althea." Cassandra joined me in front of a console table. "Althea, do you know much about Voodoo? Your mother brought you here occasionally, but I've been told you don't remember your childhood."

"Is nothing a secret around here?" I twirled a piece of my hair.

"Oh, there are many secrets here in New Orleans, especially in the paranormal community. But your arrival has stirred up all kinds of talk," Cassandra said. "I heard about your memory loss from Tasso, though."

"Tasso? Does he visit you here?" I asked.

"Oh yes. We share a fondness for seafood gumbo and gossip." Cassandra grinned. "I'm sure your mother had a good reason to block your memory. Mothers know best."

"Tell that to my daughter. She doesn't believe me when I

tell her that her new boyfriend is no good." Evangeline plopped in a chair next to a floor-to-ceiling shelf filled with old books by the looks of their spines.

"See now, I would do a spell to make him leave her alone." Cassandra poured coffee into two mugs. "But y'all are so nice that you won't do that."

"You're right, but I could do a spell that would give him a wonderful new job—in Alaska." Evangeline laughed. "But with my luck, Grace would follow him there."

"We do strange things for love—going to Alaska is the strangest thing in my book." Cassandra brought over my mug. "When your momma left for Washington, I told her she picked the most peculiar place to move to with all that cold weather. New Orleans was her home. We all missed her."

I took a sip of the coffee to give myself a moment to collect myself. My mother had friends in Seattle, but it seemed like she had left a strong community here of people who cared for her.

"I'm sorry she's no longer with us in this world." Cassandra went back to the counter and brought another mug to Evangeline. The peppermint tea had a wonderful aroma that almost tempted me to ask to try it. But the chicory coffee was just too good to put aside.

"Thank you. It's been a difficult time for the coven. A few members died recently, including Chloe," I said.

"Yes, I was sorry to hear of the loss of your older witches." Cassandra took a long sip of her coffee.

"If Chloe heard you call her an old witch, she'd show up right now screaming." Evangeline gave me a pointed look. She was turning out to be a good Dr. Watson.

"Sorry, I should have included Chloe. Even those who

are—" Cassandra paused "—abrasive, don't deserve to be murdered. Do the police have any suspects?"

"Hasn't Tasso shared the gossip with you?" I asked light-heartedly. "We know she was poisoned with ameliorate."

"Oh, that's not good for y'all. Only witches grow it. Or at least they used to." Cassandra sat in a chair by Evangeline, so I followed suit. I leaned against the high-back of the chair. The velvet fabric was worn but soft against my head.

"So you don't grow it? I see you do have some plants here," I said.

"Those are for gris gris bags, and none of them are poisonous." Cassandra crossed her legs and folded her arms.

"What are gris gris bags?" I asked.

"They are sachets that hold a special mix of herbs, oils, and stones made for a specific purpose, like warding off evil or bringing good luck," Cassandra relaxed as she explained.

"Do we have anything like that?" I turned to Evangeline.

"We carry or wear crystals, but not in pouches. I guess our lockets are the closest to gris gris bags," Evangeline said.

"Are you wearing your necklace, Althea? I remember you lost it right before you and your momma moved. She couldn't find it, no matter what spell she did. I even tried for her, but had no luck," Cassandra said.

I took the necklace out from underneath my shirt. "This is my mother's. Did you know about my lost necklace, Evangeline?"

"I vaguely remember my momma asking if I knew where you'd put yours. But you didn't hide it with me around or tell me you had lost it," Evangeline said.

"Good thing you have your mother's, then. From what I've been told, your jewelry is necessary," Cassandra said.

"Would anyone else want it? Not anyone who practices

Voodoo, of course," I added that in quickly as not to offend Cassandra again. She apparently noticed it and smiled slightly.

"I don't know. Only another paranormal would understand the necklace's true powers. I haven't heard about any bad blood between any paranormal groups as of late. In fact, the younger witches seem to hang out with the vampires," Cassandra said.

"Really? I haven't seen any of our girls at Atlas's club," Evangeline said. "Do you mean another coven's young ladies?"

"I was referring to that dive bar, Dusk. I've seen your girls, Lauren and Chloe, go in there. The newer vampires hang out there, too," Cassandra said.

"I've heard some of the older vampires do like that James Dean wannabe," Evangeline said.

"You're talking about that fool of a vampire, Trent, aren't you? Don't trust that bat, I tell you. If his lips are moving, he's lying." Cassandra shook her head.

Evangeline and I laughed. Trent didn't have friends in the paranormal community—except Madison, possibly. I stopped giggling so I could bring the conversation back to a serious tone.

"From my own experience with Trent, I wouldn't trust him either. I wonder why any of the witches would," I said.

"You should ask your young ladies. I've seen Lauren and Chloe hanging around Trent. I warned both of them to keep away from him," Cassandra said.

"They shop here?" I asked.

"Oh yes, I welcome everyone here. Ever since your coven's shop closed, this is the best place for your supplies. But I must say I miss that good food y'all made."

"We offered one hot meal a day plus to-go foods," Evangeline explained to me.

"Evangeline, your mom's pastries were so tasty." Cassandra smacked her lips. "Let me get you more tea, Evangeline."

"I'll make cinnamon rolls for you this week," Evangeline promised, and then she took a book off the shelf next to her. As she flipped the pages, Cassandra brought over her tea.

"Thanks. This is an interesting book. It's all just symbols though." Evangeline put the book on the side table where it fell open to the middle of the pages. I assumed the spine was well worn from use if it fell open to that page easily.

"Oh, I didn't realize I still had that book. I found it at ..." Cassandra said.

Cassandra and I gasped as the tea cup in Evangeline's hand crashed to the floor. The tea swirled around the shattered pieces that lay on the wood floor. I rushed over to Evangeline, who stared at the book.

"Evangeline, are you Okay? What's wrong?" I snapped my finger in front of her face to get her attention.

"I need to go." She grabbed her purse and rushed out the door, the curtain to the shop fluttering as if a hurricane had blown through.

I had only known Evangeline for a few days, but this was so unlike her. The frantic ringing of the bell on the front door meant Evangeline had left the shop altogether.

I bent down to pick up the cup pieces since I imagined Evangeline would have done the same if I were the one who left. Cassandra remained hunched over the open pages at the table.

"Cassandra, what is it? What upset Evangeline?" I placed the cup pieces on the table and stared at the pages. The page on the left was blank, and the other had an unusual drawing in black ink. It was an intricate design, but I didn't recognize it. But the Voodoo priestess did.

"This is a veve, a symbol for a loa," Cassandra said.

"What's a loa?"

"Loas are spirits we can connect with. Each one has a veve that we use when we perform rituals." Cassandra pursed her lips. "I have never seen this one before. It's a variation of Baron Samdi's veve."

"Who is that? And why would Evangeline be so upset by it?"

The symbol was drawn in blocks, three tiers of rectangles forming the base of a cross. Inside these images were wavy lines that seemed random. Outside this primary image were four elongated hexagons, which I would guess were coffins. Especially when I peered closer and discovered a tiny skull in the center of each one. The drawing was peculiar but not sinister. But when I ran a finger over it, a wave of nausea hit me.

"What's wrong, Althea?" Cassandra asked when I jerked my finger away.

"Something isn't right about that book. Run your finger over the veve."

Cassandra did, but she didn't jerk her finger away like I did. She closed her eyes and began chanting words I couldn't understand. I considered running away like Evangeline, but Cassandra returned to normal in less than thirty seconds.

"I agree. This book is meant for evil. I don't know who or for what purpose yet, but I will find out." Cassandra's voice was powerful, but her hand shook as she placed the book down on the side table.

"Who is Baron Samedi and why would they make a knock-off of his veve?" I said.

"He's in charge of the crossroads of the living and the dead for our community. We use his veve in rituals regarding the living and the dead. I assume it's similar to rituals your covens do."

"I haven't done one yet, but I'll take your word for it."

"I keep forgetting you just returned." Cassandra sank into the chair, so I sat across from her. "Althea, I came across this book at a flea market in Houma five years ago. I only flipped through the first few pages when I realized it was full of veves and old rituals. Nothing seemed wrong about it, so I put the book on the shelf to look through later. I never did."

"Evangeline recognized that symbol for somewhere. Would it be used in witchcraft?"

"I hope not. Changing a veve like that tells me someone is up to no good. If both you and I can feel the evil rising from it, someone has strong powers out there."

"By the cracking on the spine, I'd say the original owner used that symbol a lot. What kind of ritual would you do with them?"

"I have no idea." Cassandra pushed herself out of the chair as if she had aged ten years. "Let me get something to clean this up with."

When her back was toward me, I took out my cell phone and snapped pictures of the veve. I looked through the entire book and the cover, but there were no clues to the owner or where it came from.

"You better go to Evangeline and make sure she's all right. Tell her to see me when she's ready." Cassandra swept the shards into a plastic wastebasket. "I want to assure her I don't practice black magic, and I want to uncover the truth together."

"I'll let her know." I gathered my purse and headed

toward the curtain, but stopped when Cassandra called out to me.

"Take care of yourself. Something is off-kilter in our world. Protect yourself and your coven." She put down the wastebasket and walked over to me.

"You be careful, too." I couldn't move. It was as if Cassandra's tense gaze kept me in place.

"Althea, let me tell you this as one priestess to another. If anyone in the Voodoo community wanted to kill a witch, we wouldn't use your plant. We have easier and untraceable ways."

The coffee in my stomach churned, and I gulped in a breath to keep from being sick.

"I don't say this to be threatening or to prove my innocence to you." Cassandra's voice softened as she placed a hand gently on my cheek. "I can tell you have a good soul and are as powerful as your momma and her momma before her."

"Thank you," I whispered as tears welled in my eyes. The emotion that overcame me was unexpected and confusing.

"You have a tough road ahead, but stay strong." She took her hand from my cheek. "It's your place in this world to lead your coven. But you can't do it if you're dead."

With that, Cassandra left me and stood in front of her altar and lit a new candle. As she bowed her head and placed her hands on the skull, I backed out of the room. I ran to the front door and flung it open, wishing I was leaving behind my fears and doubts about my future with the coven... and my life.

33

Evangeline leaned against a streetlight with her eyes closed and her arms hugging her body. I put my hand on her shoulder and she jumped and yelped.

"It's me! It's Okay." I took a step back to give her space.

"Thank goodness it's you!" Evangeline threw her arms around me and squeezed me tight. Her body stopped shaking after a few moments, and she pulled away from me.

"Althea, I'm so sorry I left you there. I didn't know what else to do."

"What spooked you? Did you recognize the symbol in the book?" I said.

"Yes. Why would my husband have a Voodoo symbol in his journals?"

I didn't know what to say, since I had no clue either.

"Okay, we need to talk. Do you want to get coffee?" I asked.

"No, this calls for a drink. Follow me."

Evangeline hustled down the street, and I ran after her. I

didn't bother to ask where we were going since it didn't matter. Her whole body radiated with a frantic energy, so I doubted she would stop to answer a simple question.

We reached the Hotel Monteleone a few blocks away. Evangeline threw the door open before the doorman reached it. I followed her to a carousel. Yes, a carousel. I stopped and stared.

At least it looked like a carousel with a round platform that slowly rotated a circle of seats that faced the center. Just like a regular carousel, the top was decorated with alternating mirrors and three-dimensional jester faces, surrounded by bright lights. What differed here were the shelves of glasses and bottles on the center pole and that the seats were not carved animals but barstools.

Evangeline was a few steps ahead of me, but she turned to face me.

"Oh my, I forgot you haven't been here before!" Evangeline's face relaxed and she giggled. "This is the Carousel Bar, which is aptly named as you see. Don't worry, this is as fast as it goes."

"Please tell me the chairs don't go up and down."

"Only if you have too many Vieux Carrés." She reached back and grabbed my hand. "Come on, you're going to love this place."

Evangeline took a seat on a zebra-painted chair on the merry-go-round. I took the lion chair next to her, thankful that these were stools and not animal shaped seats. But it moved like a real carousel.

"Don't worry, it takes fifteen minutes to go around so you won't fly out of your chair," the bartender said. "What can I get you ladies?"

"I need a Vieux Carré," Evangeline said.

"What's that?" I said.

"It's our signature cocktail. It's rye whiskey, Bénédictine, cognac, sweet vermouth, and bitters," the bartender said.

"That's too much liquor for me, especially this early. No offense, Evangeline," I said.

"None taken." Evangeline patted my hand. "I doubt any of your Seattle bars offered it."

"Oh, you're from Seattle. Welcome to New Orleans. I'm Ben, your bartender and guide to all New Orleans drinks," he said. "How about a Sazerac?"

I shook my head. "No, thanks. Let's go with a Bloody Mary."

"Of course, but maybe I can get you to try something new for your next round." Ben smiled and moved a few feet down the bar to prepare our drinks.

"Are you ready to talk?"

"What? Sorry, no. Let's get our drinks first, and then I promise to explain." Evangeline tore a cocktail napkin into even shreds.

While she did that, I snapped a few photos to send to Olivia. I got down from my stool and walked around the carousel. I returned to my seat as Ben placed our drinks in front of us.

"Enjoy ladies. I'm at your service when you're ready." Ben gave a little bow and went to greet a couple who sat on the other side of the carousel.

Evangeline sipped her drink and then let out a long sigh. "I needed that. Thanks for being so patient, Thea. Now let me do a spell so we can talk." She closed her eyes and said, "In secrecy, our words will hold sway, Only whispers of weather, we'll convey."

I looked around the room, expecting a change. There wasn't one.

"What did that do?" I asked.

"No one can understand what we're saying. They'll hear us talking about the weather."

"Witches are like spies." I laughed. "We can hide what we're doing and mask what we're saying. That'd be pretty useful in espionage."

"I imagine most covert operations are done by witches." Evangeline grinned, but her expression changed to a frown. "I wish I was a secret agent so I could find out what happened to my husband."

"We're witches, so there's no need to be a spy. Tell me everything about your husband's disappearance."

Through the tears, Evangeline shared her story. Bryce acted oddly for six months before he disappeared. At first, Evangeline thought he was having an affair, but she didn't find any proof. When she confronted him, he laughed and assured her it was just a midlife crisis.

"But for the next few months, he stayed away from home more and more. He claimed he was working late, but I did a location spell." Evangeline began shredding another napkin. "He wasn't at his office, but I couldn't find him. It takes a strong paranormal to block that spell."

"Was Bryce paranormal at all?" I said.

"No. One reason I fell in love with him was he was just a regular guy. He didn't care that I was a witch."

"So he knew you were a witch and still married you? There's hope for me, yet." I wanted to lighten the mood as Evangeline's tears returned.

She wiped away her tears with a non-shredded napkin and smiled. But I could see through her mask. Her heartbreak remained as intense as the day Bryce vanished. In all my time with Evangeline, I considered her the happiest person I'd ever met. Now I understood she hid her pain behind her perky disposition.

"I thought we were happy until he disappeared. Bryce left for his office like usual. He owned his own accounting firm," Evangeline said.

"I assume he didn't come home from work." I paused as Evangeline nodded. "Did he leave a note?"

"He did, but I suspected he didn't write it."

"Why not?"

"It looked like his handwriting, but the phrases weren't how he spoke. The letter said to go on without him and travel to Egypt and ride the camels like I always wanted to do." Evangeline crinkled her nose. "Bryce knew I never wanted to ride a camel."

"That sounds like he was sending you a message."

"I couldn't decide which way to take it. Either he hated me and wanted me to do things I hated..." Evangeline put her hand up to her lips.

"Or he was trying to tell you he wrote the note under duress." I finished her thought for her. "Now, what does the Voodoo symbol have to do with his disappearance?"

Evangeline gripped the edge of the bar. Her knuckles turned white. "After he was missing for five months, my daughter and I cleaned out his office. Underneath a stack of accounting books, I found a notebook. Most of the pages were full of random numbers, then came pages of strange symbols."

"Did you recognize any of them? Besides the one in the Voodoo book, of course."

"No. Some were like the Voodoo one, but others were just odd drawings. I didn't touch it like I did with the one today. I put it aside thinking I'd get back to it later. But I never did."

"You had to take care of yourself and your daughter." I put my arm around Evangeline, and she rested her head on my shoulder. "What do you want to do now? We can go back and talk to Priestess Cassandra…"

Evangeline shook her head. "Until I'm sure the evil symbol is the one in Bryce's book, let's keep this to ourselves. I've never had any reason not to trust her, but I want to be careful."

"I understand. Do you think Bryce was practicing Voodoo?"

"I can't imagine that he would. But then again, I didn't expect him to disappear."

"So what's your plan?" I asked.

"I'll go to my storage unit in Hammond. His things are there and I need that book. I need answers."

"I completely understand, Evangeline. Do what you need to do. When you get back, I'll help you find out what happened to your husband."

Evangeline sat up straight. "I'm so happy you're back, Thea. You and I will figure this out, won't we?"

I handed her a napkin. "Of course we will. We'll be the middle-aged Nancy Drews of the French Quarter."

We laughed so much that the bartender came over and brought us two fresh drinks. "Not sure if you ladies need more to drink, but y'all's laughter is making me as happy as a pig in a pile of mud."

"That's mighty kind of you, Ben. I bet you see all kinds of people acting foolish." Evangeline's Southern accent grew thicker.

"Yes, I do. But I've never heard two beautiful women giggle so much about the weather." Ben winked and went to a group of four who sat down at the carousel.

"Do you think he knows we're witches?" I twirled a piece

of my hair. "He winked about the weather. Does everyone know we have a spell that sounds like we're talking about the weather?"

"Honey, don't you worry about who knows what spells we do. I imagine some people might have figured it out, but I bet he was just flirting with you."

"Oh, please. He's like twenty years younger than me. I could be his mother." I rolled my eyes.

"I'd tell you to get his number, but Atlas is more your type."

I gulped my drink hard, which made me cough. "I'm not looking for a relationship with anyone, especially a vampire."

"So you say." Evangeline smirked. "You're the coven leader, so you could allow witches to date vampires."

"Luella should stay as the head of the coven. I'm not leadership material."

"I beg to differ, but I'll drop it for now." Evangeline pulled her wallet out of her purse. "I have two meetings coming up. I can't cancel them, so I'll go to the storage unit after that."

"Would you like me to come with you?"

"No, I can do this on my own. But I'll need your help when I come back with that book."

"I'll be waiting for you."

"Thanks, Thea." Evangeline wrung her hands. "Bryce broke my heart by leaving, but now I have to really wonder if he didn't leave on his own."

We silently waited for the bartender to bring our check. Evangeline was biting the lipstick off her lips, so I imagined she was thinking about every little detail of her husband's disappearance. For a moment, I considered insisting I come along with her.

But then I remembered my own mysteries that I needed to solve. I would be no help to Evangeline if I were in jail for Chloe's murder.

34

After paying our check and leaving a generous tip for our bartender, we waited outside the hotel. The doorman waved down a cab for Evangeline.

"I plan to leave for Hammond around five. It shouldn't take long to find the notebook, so I should be back here by seven thirty." Evangeline tipped the doorman and then slid into the back of the cab.

I leaned inside and said, "If you don't call or text me by eight, I'm coming to find you."

"Darling, you don't need to come after me. You're a witch! Do a spell!" Evangeline cackled as I stepped back and let the doorman close the cab door.

If the doorman overheard Evangeline, he ignored it and wished me a good afternoon. The walk back to Fontenot Mansion took about fifteen minutes, giving me time to think. When Evangeline reminded me I was a witch, a sense of amazement came over me. In just a few days, I had become a witch who read minds, made flowers grow, and talked to her deceased mother.

But becoming a witch didn't come without its problems.

I still remembered nothing about my childhood here. My mother wasn't happy I came back. And the worst part were the murders.

Finding Chloe's killer would clear my name. Was Chloe's killer the same person who murdered my mother and the other witches? I only had my intuition to rely on until I found the proof.

Now there was the mystery of Evangeline's husband to resolve. I couldn't forget the mystery of the ritual my mother performed that made her leave town. While I was at it, I might as well try to find out who my father is. What's another mystery to solve?

My head throbbed as I reached my house. I needed to go through all this information swirling in my mind. I unlocked the gate to the courtyard instead of the front entrance. Sitting in the warm sunshine with the soothing sounds of the water fountain would be the perfect place to work through my thoughts.

Someone else had the same idea.

Tasso was lying on a slate tile in the courtyard, sunning himself. I was tempted to join him and pretend to be a cat, too. I wish I only had to think about eating and napping.

"Hello, Tasso." I sat on a chair next to him.

He opened one eye and meowed.

"Nice to see you, too." I inhaled the sweet scent of jasmine that cascaded down the brick a few feet away from me. Being able to sit outside comfortably in February was such a treat. In the Pacific Northwest it would be cold, raining, or snowing. Actually, it could be all three.

"Is the weather always this good here?"

Tasso stood up and stretched his front legs forward. "You're not going to stop talking, so I better get up. No, the weather isn't always this way. Wait until the summer. You'll be sweating like a sinner in church."

"I'll just leave before then."

"Thea-Bea, don't say that. You just got here. What's wrong with New Orleans?" Tasso appeared agitated, swishing his tail.

"The only things wrong so far are Chloe's murder and almost being mugged by a vampire." There were things that were right, like my friendship with Evangeline, the food, and Atlas. But being a murder suspect and an almost victim of a vampire carried more weight.

"I'll give you that, but otherwise, I bet you like it here. New Orleans gets in your soul and doesn't let you go, no matter how far away you are."

"You should work for the tourism board," I said.

"Nah, I got things to do." Tasso sauntered over to the chair across from mine and jumped into it. "I can tell your mind is working overtime. What's going on? Any news about Chloe's murder? And how are things with your momma?"

"I haven't heard anything from Knox, but I have some information I've gathered with Evangeline."

Tasso sat attentively as I recounted the visit to the Bordelon Coven's shop and Madison's attempted hexing. He twitched his nose when I told him about Trent and Madison's interaction in front of the bar.

"Hold it. Lauren was there, too? What's one of our witches doing at that bar?" Tasso interrupted me when I recounted seeing Lauren at the bar as well.

"Maybe she was only there for a drink."

"By the tone of your voice, I'd say you don't believe that," Tasso said.

"Do you think Lauren had something to do with Chloe's death?"

"I hope not, but Chloe tormented that poor girl. What else did you find out?"

"Seraphine Bordelon hinted that the Voodoo community had something to do with Chloe's death."

Tasso meowed and jumped off the chair. "Did she now? Well, ain't that something? Did she offer any proof?"

"No, she only alluded to it. Do you think Priestess Cassandra could have something to do with Chloe's murder? Or even the deaths of my mom and the other witches?"

Tasso paced in front of me, his tail hitting my legs as he did. I let him be until he was ready to talk. I rested my eyes, letting the fading sun warm my face. After walking past me at least twenty times, Tasso meowed.

"Now, Thea-Bea, I have nothing against the Voodoo group. But even though Seraphine is supposed to be the be-all and end-all of witches..."

"Oh, really?"

"Don't interrupt me, child," Tasso snapped. "I don't trust her farther than I can throw a hairball. There's something off about her. But maybe that's just me."

"Atlas trusts her."

"Oh, and you don't like that, do you?" Tasso laughed. "Didn't Luella give you the romance rules for witches?"

My face burned, not just from the sun. "We are friends and it will stay that way. Let's get back to the business at hand. Would another coven or Priestess Cassandra have a reason to kill our witches?"

"Ain't that the million-dollar question? Power, money, revenge are the popular motives, right? The Fontenot witches are the strongest women and have been since your great-great-great-great-great grandmother started this coven right here in this courtyard."

Tasso trotted to the fountain, and I followed him. I sat on the edge and dipped my hand in the water. The cool water sent a shiver up my arm. Tasso jumped up next to me and put a paw on my leg.

"Listen, I know Luella thinks your momma and the other witches were murdered. I brushed her off, but now I might agree with her. All that stuff you've found out about the Bordelon Coven and Trent makes me wonder."

I scratched Tasso under his chin, more for my comfort than his. All the sassiness and confidence seemed to have left his body. I didn't intend to stress him out, but his concern validated mine. And Luella's, it seemed.

"So what now? Should I talk to Knox?" I twisted my hair so hard that I jerked my head.

"Cher, don't pull your hair out." Tasso's voice softened. "Let's talk this out."

I sat up straight and exhaled deeply. "We know that Chloe's tea was poisoned with a plant only witches grow and her locket was stolen."

"Has anyone found Chloe's locket?"

"The key to this mystery must be the locket, or rather, lockets. Luella and Evangeline believe the necklaces have been stolen. Whether they're for someone to use or weaken the covent, nobody knows," I said.

"That's a lead you should hunt down like a fat cat chasing a slow mouse."

"I thought you didn't like to be called fat." I couldn't help but laugh.

"It's just an idiom, Thea. But really, whatcha going to do now?" Tasso yawned. "Sorry, I haven't gotten my twenty hours of sleep yet."

"Twenty hours? I wish I was a cat." I laughed.

"No, you don't." Tasso's voice grew serious. "Not all cats have it easy, but that tale, no pun intended, is for another day. Get going and solve this mess. No more witches should die."

I picked Tasso up and held him over my shoulder. He settled into me, so he didn't seem to mind me treating him like a regular cat. His soft fur and the low rumble of his purring comforted me. When I placed him back on the ground, he cleaned his eyes with his paws.

"So, Althea, the detective, what are you going to do now?"

"I'm going to find a vampire."

35

———

I rushed out of the courtyard before Tasso asked me which vampire I needed to find. If I caught Trent with Chloe's locket, Knox would have to investigate him. That was if Knox believed me when I shared my observation of Trent and Madison together.

As I started toward Atlas's club, the sun shined in my eyes, so I pulled out my sunglasses. Then it hit me. Neither Atlas nor Trent would be around just yet. I checked the weather app on my cell phone to find that sunset would be around 5:45 p.m. I had about thirty minutes to kill. Okay, not the best phrase to use.

Before I could figure out what to do, Luella turned the corner, heading toward me. She didn't notice me until she was a few feet away.

"Althea, I'm glad you're here." The seriousness on her face worried me. "Tonight we're having a memorial for Chloe. It's just for coven members."

"Oh, that's a nice thing to do," I stammered. Was I expected to be there? I wanted to honor Chloe, but I sensed some witches wouldn't welcome me.

And I was right.

Luella tilted her head from side to side as she breathed in deeply. I didn't need the powers of ESP to see that she wasn't sure what to say to me.

"Some of the coven don't want me at the memorial," I stated calmly. To most of the group, I was still an outsider, a stranger, and even Chloe's killer.

"Yes, I'm sorry. I had hoped everyone would put aside their feelings to include you..." Luella's voice faded.

"It's Okay. They'll change their minds as soon as I clear my name."

"Yes, that will help."

"But? I sense there is a but."

She nodded. "There is concern about the mansion and the future of our coven. Have you given it any more thought?"

I made sure I had blocked my mind, as I didn't want Luella to hear my thoughts. So many ideas ran through my head, and I didn't want to give her false hope. While New Orleans had its charms, I didn't know if I wanted to be a witch here. I couldn't decide until my name was off Knox's suspect list.

"No, Luella, I haven't decided what I'm doing with the house yet. Until Chloe's killer is caught, my hands are tied," I said.

"Fair enough. The memorial will be in the courtyard at eight p.m. We'll start setting up an hour beforehand." Luella brushed her hand on my arm as she passed me. "If you want to come, I'll make sure no one bothers you."

I shook my head. "I think it's best if I stay away this evening."

"What will you do?" Luella stared at me like a parent wondering if their teenager was going to a keg party.

"I'll be a tourist and go listen to music and eat gumbo," I said.

"You're not going to see Atlas?"

"I might go by the club for a drink."

"Whatever you do, stay out of trouble. You're wearing your necklace, aren't you?"

I pulled out the necklace from under my shirt. "Happy now?"

"Yes. We should be done around ten, so don't stay out too late." Luella came back over to me and hugged me. "I'm sorry about all this. You'll be one hundred percent part of the coven soon."

She rushed up to the gate and hurried up the stairs. Luella had a powerful evening ahead of her. And so did I.

Listening to music and eating gumbo would have been fun, but I needed to find Knox. I doubted he would welcome my theories on Chloe's murder, but I didn't care. The information I'd gathered on Madison and Trent needed to be shared.

I called his cell phone, but it went to voicemail. I didn't want to leave my information as a message, so I started toward the police station. The sky changed from blue to yellow to orange the farther I walked. The sky's colors paled compared to the outfits people were wearing on Royal Street.

Those wearing layers of gold, green, and purple beads were the least dramatically dressed people. The first unusual group I came upon was a quartet of aliens. Yes, four people wearing head-to-toe green alien costumes. Their alien face masks were pushed up on top of their heads as they drank from to-go cups.

Next, was a walking solar system. A group of eight each wore a round ball that covered almost their entire bodies. They even painted their faces to match the planet they represented.

Both groups, plus other random people, dressed in space costumes, characters from sci-fi movies and television shows, and robot outfits, headed in the same direction. My curiosity got the best of me, so I followed them at least until I reached the police station. I was swept up in the joy and laughter of everyone on the streets, in costume or not. People stopped for photos with each other and exchanged beads. As I reached for my cell phone, I was tapped on the shoulder. I turned around.

"Detective Dupriest?"

Knox wasn't dressed in his suit and tie, but in a robot costume. It reminded me of the one I made for my daughter when she was ten. We spent weeks painting boxes in silver and adding buttons and Christmas lights to turn her into a bright and cheerful robot. Knox's costume appeared professionally made, with sounds and lights emitting from it.

"Good evening, Miss Fontenot. You seemed perplexed." Knox's silver make-up didn't crack as he smiled. "Tonight is the Chewbacchus parade. As you might have guessed, it is a science fiction themed parade."

"Oh, the costumes make sense now." I laughed. "Are you in the parade or an enthusiastic bystander?"

"I'm in the parade, although I'm running late. Some new information came in."

I didn't like the way Knox looked at me. "I assume you're not going to arrest someone in that costume."

"No. But I was going to speak with you tomorrow. Why don't you walk with me and we can chat casually about it?"

"Talk casually? What does that mean?" My pulse raced, and we hadn't even started walking.

"I mean, this is off the record. We can talk officially tomorrow. Unless you'd like to confess."

"No, I have nothing to confess to about Chloe," I insisted.

"All right. Do you have anything else to confess, then?" Knox looked serious, except for a slight smile.

"I'll confess I've never seen anything as wild as this." I went with humor and hoped I had read Knox correctly.

"Just wait until the parade is in full swing. I need to go to my krewe's starting place. Would you still like to walk and talk?"

"Let's go." I followed Knox down the street, weaving in and out of the crowds. We turned down Dumaine, which wasn't as busy.

"Miss Fontenot, by chance were you coming to see me when we ran into each other?" Knox asked.

"I was. There are things you should know about Chloe."

"If you are talking about her interactions with Priestess Cassandra, I am aware of them. I followed up on purchases Chloe made there, as well as at Tea, Tarot, and Truth."

Knox looked straight ahead, so I couldn't get much of a read on his face from the side. Once again, I couldn't read his mind.

"Oh. Did you learn anything?"

"I found out you and Evangeline Cormier have been to both stores." Knox stopped walking and faced me. "Were you channeling your inner Jessica Fletcher?"

"No..."

"Nancy Drew, then? Ms. Fontenot, you haven't struck me

as the type of woman who would lie to the police. Please don't start now."

I crossed my arms and glared at him. I couldn't afford to lie if I wanted him to take my information seriously. I plastered on a smile and said, "At least you didn't refer to me as Miss Marple. Fine, I was curious about the Voodoo community and the Bordelon Coven."

"Go on." Knox pointed to an empty wall in between two shops. We stood against the brick wall. "Tell me what you learned."

I recounted my interactions with Priestess Cassandra and Madison. He kept a straight face until I mentioned seeing Trent and Madison together, exchanging an envelope. I described Madison trying to grab whatever was on the end of Trent's pocket chain.

"I didn't realize Trent had any friends in the witch community," Knox said. "Although Dusk is popular with young paranormals. I've heard your fellow witches Chloe Chase and Lauren Shaw went there."

My heart sank for Lauren. Did Knox consider her a strong suspect for Chloe's murder?

"Lauren wouldn't murder another witch," I said.

"But the poison was from a plant that witches grow."

"There are tons of witches in this town!" I threw my hands up in the air.

"You're one of them now," Knox said matter-of-factly.

"Yes..." I paused as an idea hit me. "But I wasn't when Chloe was murdered. I didn't even know about the special plants witches grew."

"I'll take that under advisement, but I must say that's just your word. Yes, I'll talk to Miss Lulu," Knox said. "Powers or not, you have ownership of Fontenot Mansion."

"I already told you that at the police station."

"At the time you met Chloe in person, did you know she had spoken to a lawyer about stopping any potential sale of the house?"

I bit my lip so I wouldn't rant that Chloe had no right to do that. It didn't matter what she had done, except now it was a motive for me to have killed her. At least in Knox's eyes.

"The attorney gave me a copy of the letter he sent to you."

"I never got a letter. I swear. I had no idea that Chloe had met with a lawyer about the house."

"I appreciate you talking to me tonight. I'll be in touch soon."

He moved, but I touched his arm to get his attention.

"Knox, I mean Detective Dupriest, I had no reason to kill Chloe. And remember, I just became a witch a few days ago."

"Althea, I mean Ms. Fontenot. I take everything into consideration. But I need proof, not innuendos." He was stone-faced. He must be great at poker.

"I understand. Have fun at your parade." I faked a smile to hide my dejection.

Knox nodded and left me alone, more worried than I was before.

36

I leaned back against the wall as the crowds surged past me. "Cheer up, darling! It's time for a parade!" a man wearing antenna ears shouted at me as he danced by me.

Should I go to the parade? I didn't want to go back home although I could hide in my room during the memorial. When a group of women dressed as witches with light-up swords walked past me, I had to laugh. Were they genuine witches mocking the situation, or just a group of women having fun? I read the mind of the last one in line and learned they weren't witches, and that they were late getting to their spot in the parade.

"Excuse me, can you tell me the parade route? I'm a tourist," I asked the witch. It seemed wrong to keep digging in her brain for simple information.

"Sure! It starts in the Marigny on St. Claude Street and turns on Decatur Street to end in the French Quarter." She stepped closer to me and whispered, "Honey, don't announce that you're a tourist. You don't want someone to try to pickpocket you. Especially if you're drinking."

"Thanks." I put my purse over my body cross-wise and she smiled.

"Good. Head to the Marigny for the best viewing spots. Would you like to join us? We have an extra sword."

"I can't, but thank you." I held back my laughter, imagining myself as a genuine witch in a parade with fake ones.

After she left, I took out my phone to check the map. A text from Evangeline popped up: *I'm Okay. It's taking longer to get through all these boxes. I'll text you when I find it.*

I sent a thumbs-up emoji back instead of blowing up her phone about my conversation with Knox. Evangeline had enough to worry about without me dumping on her. But I wished she were here with me. Going to the parade alone didn't seem fun, but what else could I do? Of course, now that it was dark, Atlas should be at his club. Should I go to the parade or the club?

Someone else made that decision for me. I spotted a vampire in the crowd. No, not a sci-fi vampire, but a real one.

Trent sauntered down the street, just dressed as his normal fifties' style attire. He appeared to be chatting up two young women, not wearing costumes either. They were heading toward the parade route and now I was, too.

Evangeline and I had joked that witches would make excellent spies, so that's what I became. I stayed twenty feet behind Trent and his apparent new friends as they headed toward the Marigny, which I discovered was the neighborhood next to the French Quarter. If I hadn't been spying on Trent, I would have slowed down to take in the brightly colored cottages and their owners sitting on their porches waving at people.

They settled on the corner of Elysian Fields and Royal Street instead of going to the start of the parade. Washington Park was behind them, and they stood against the fence. I waited across the street on the other side of Royal to see what Trent would do. So far, he and the women appeared to be chatting and waiting for the parade to start.

Could this just be an innocent outing for Trent? My intuition said no. I needed to get closer to them without Trent seeing me. I crossed the street and for the next twenty minutes, I stood ten feet down from him. Standing near two tall, muscular, and beer-smelling men wasn't ideal, but it worked. Trent focused on the women and never turned my way.

Just when I decided I couldn't take the smell of beer any longer, Trent made his move.

As the floats approached, the woman on his right pushed her way to the sidewalk. The bright lights of a six-foot-wide UFO surrounded by aliens throwing beads was one of the silliest things I had seen, but I loved it. It would have been great to enjoy the revelry, but I couldn't. Trent shifted his attention to the woman who stayed with him. He stared at her, not making a sound. Was he mesmerizing her? Or was he going to bite her? I couldn't let that happen.

I started toward him but stopped as soon as I saw him slip the bracelet from her wrist. It was made entirely of deep purple crystals. Could it be the tanzanite? I needed to get closer to see it, but should I reveal myself yet? A photo would be better to show Knox, so I took my cell phone out and snapped a photo of Trent holding the bracelet. Granted, it only proved he was a thief, but it was a start. I zoomed in on Trent, and sure enough, it looked like the same type of crystal. If so, it must have cost a fortune since the necklace was so expensive at the Bordelon shop. Why did Trent need such powerful crystals?

She faced the street with glazed-over eyes. While putting away the bracelet, Trent also took out his chain. I almost dropped my phone when I saw what hung on the end of his chain.

A silver locket with a jasmine flower glinted under the gaslight. I snapped photo after photo while Trent put it away. I needed to confirm if Chloe's family name was on her necklace. This must have been what Madison wanted from Trent the other night. Was he keeping it for himself or to sell to a higher bidder than Madison? Why would Madison want it?

Sending the pictures to Knox or Luella would have been logical. They were both busy, and I had no proof until I saw the necklace up close. My anger pushed logic aside. I wanted to find out why Trent stole the necklace and, most likely, killed Chloe. And then I needed to find Madison. I bet she gave Trent the poison to put in Chloe's cup.

First things first, I had to follow Trent. He whispered in the woman's ear and then snapped his fingers. I couldn't hear what she said to Trent, but she left him and joined her friend. She didn't seem to notice her bracelet was missing. I weaved through the crowds after Trent crossed Royal Street.

My heart sank as he left the parade route. How could I follow him without him catching me? I held my breath as I inched along the buildings, hoping he wouldn't see me in the shadows. Fortunately, he only went three blocks before turning onto Spain Street. Two blocks later he stopped in front of a warehouse. He banged on the door and Madison opened it and ushered him inside. I didn't need to be a witch to know they were up to no good in that building.

But I needed my witch skills to get inside. I had a plan.

37

Opening my grimoire, I searched for spells to help me get inside. There might be a spell on the building keeping me from entering, but I wouldn't know unless I tried. Sure enough, a spell existed to unlock doors sealed by other witches. On wobbly legs, I walked up to the warehouse door. I placed my hand on the cold doorknob, which vibrated. It didn't hurt, but I registered the change in the surrounding atmosphere.

I cleared my throat and said, "Ancestors, I ask you to unlock this door in my hour of need. No harm to the witch who sealed it, I decree. What's hidden within, reveal to me."

Two locks clicked. I turned the knob, and the door opened. I entered a dark hallway and shut the door behind me.

The linoleum-lined hallway was silent as I tiptoed, with no voices or noise to be heard. I glimpsed an office to my left with a see-through window. A plain metal desk had a phone on it, and shelves lined the walls. Some were empty and others had notebooks in them. I couldn't read anything on the spines of the books, so I kept going.

Five feet down the way, a door labeled "Supplies" appeared. I repeated my spell, and the door opened. At first I only saw rolls of paper towels and stacks of copier paper. Beyond that, I saw a shelf with handwritten notes on brown boxes. The boxes were labeled "Candles," "Tarot Cards," and "Bagged Tea" showed they were inventory for a shop. The shipping label was addressed to Tea, Tarot and Truth. This was a Bordelon warehouse.

I left the supply room and headed toward a large door in the hallway. Were Trent and Madison in there? They had nowhere else to go.

I had no idea what was behind the door. Did I have a spell for X-ray vision? The answer was no after I flipped through my grimoire. But when Luella restored my powers, she performed the incantation that made us invisible. I couldn't find it in my grimoire, but I was pretty sure I had it memorized. It was worth the risk.

I whispered, "Let us be invisible to the world as we perform our sacred spell. Keep us safe from prying eyes until we are ready to reveal our true selves."

I hoped I did it right. The only way to see if it worked was to enter the room and go near Trent and Madison. For a moment, I considered calling Knox, but telling him I was breaking and entering wouldn't go over well. And as he said, he needed proof, not innuendos.

I took in a deep breath and cautiously opened the door.

38

I opened the door wide enough to slip inside. Racks from floor to ceiling filled the large room. Some boxes were marked with shop inventory, but many file boxes remained unmarked. When I put my hand on one, a jolt of energy went up my arm. I tried it on another box and it happened again. I tried the open-door spell on the box, but it wouldn't open no matter how much I tried lifting the lid. Either they were sealed with extremely strong tape or there was a spell on them.

I went to another shelf when I heard Madison and Trent arguing. Knox wanted proof, so I turned on the voice recorder on my phone. I slipped it in my jacket pocket and hoped the recording would be good enough for Knox. Not feeling quite confident about my cloaking spell, I just leaned my head out.

They stood facing each other at a long metal table with a file box on it. Madison's face was flushed, and she was shaking her finger in Trent's face. He had his arms crossed and scowled at Madison.

"Listen, Trent. We have the money. Give us the necklace."

"Here's the crystal bracelet you wanted, but no locket until I get more money." Trent slammed down the bracelet he stole from the woman at the parade on the table. "I'm taking a bigger risk now that the police are on to Chloe's death. More risk means more money, sugar."

"But we agreed on the price!" Madison squealed.

"It's not my fault you picked poison to kill Chloe. Maybe if you had made it look like an accident, that stupid were-wolf wouldn't be poking into everyone's business."

"You're the one that said it would look like an accident! Why else would I trust you with the tea? And you haven't even used it on..." Madison stopped talking and looked around the room. I stepped behind the shelf in case my spell hadn't worked.

It had not.

"Is that you, Althea Fontenot? If you did a cloaking spell, it failed!" Madison shouted.

Great, I messed up the spell. I was positive I said the right words. Oh, I didn't have the jasmine flowers! That might have been it, but it didn't matter now.

Should I run and escape through the door? Could I outrun Madison and Trent to the front door? Trent didn't give me that chance to try. He changed into a bat and flew toward me. He landed on the floor but changed back into human form.

"Let's have a chat, Althea." Trent's fangs looked sharper and bigger tonight.

"Yes, let's talk," I said.

Trent walked back to the table where Madison waited. As I strode to them, I tried to keep my face blank and my mind blocked in case Madison tried to read it. If I acted like

I wasn't scared, I hoped I could get myself out of this mess —alive.

"Althea, you're not very good at tailing a person. I knew you were at the parade. Did you enjoy seeing me work? I had planned to give my new friend a bite, but I guessed you would have stopped me."

I gulped down the stomach acid that climbed up my throat. Apparently, I wasn't a good spy or witch.

"I can't believe you were hiding back there. You're supposed to be this high-and-mighty witch, but obviously not." Madison giggled, but there was fear in her eyes. I focused on that.

"I may be out of practice, but you believe the Fontenot witches are the strongest. Is that why you're killing witches and stealing the lockets?"

"See, I told you someone would figure it out." Madison slapped Trent's arm. "Give me the locket now and I can try to kill her."

The fear of dying helped me keep my composure. "You need the locket to kill me? But you didn't get the lockets from everyone that died."

"But I didn't—"

Trent put his hand over Madison's mouth. "Stop talking, Madison. You don't owe Althea any information. But we need to figure out a way to kill her that isn't suspicious."

I tried to stall them from coming up with my death plan. "Why did you kill Chloe? I heard you three were friends. People say you were together at Dusk."

"Did Lauren tell you that? She should die next." Trent groaned. "She's got a big mouth for a woman with a mousy personality."

"What does it matter if we hung out? Chloe and I were friends," Madison said.

"She wasn't involved in your schemes?" I hoped Chloe hadn't been involved.

Trent cackled, which sent a shiver down my spine. "Chloe was all about herself. She wanted power, and boy, was she mad when you came to town."

"But she didn't kill anyone in your coven. Chloe wanted to run your coven. She wanted as much tanzanite as she could get. She wanted to do more powerful spells." Madison sounded almost sorry for Chloe.

"But why did you kill her?" I asked. "She was a fellow witch. Shouldn't all witches support each other, even if they're in different covens?"

Trent sighed. "I'm so bored with all this witch stuff. You women just want power and then you do nothing with it. If I had your power, I'd take over this town, this state, the country!"

"What's in this for you, Trent? Do you hate my coven so much you'll steal necklaces and crystals for her?" Madison's eyes quickly shifted toward a door in the back of the room as I pointed at her. "Where does that door lead to? Is someone else here?"

Madison's face dropped, along with any confidence she had. "Trent, she'll be here soon, so we need to take care of things or else..."

"Stop being so scared. Do some witchy thing on her then!" Trent banged his fists on the table.

"Don't order me around! But I'll do it." Madison put on the tanzanite bracelet and walked up to me. She raised her hands in the air and yelled, "I call upon my ancestors to strike down this witch once and for all. Stop her before she is the reason for our coven's downfall."

"Is that it? Why isn't she dead?" Trent said.

"Sorry, Madison, but I have a protection spell on me. No

one in your coven can harm me." I tossed my hair over my shoulder, hoping I appeared confident. Now I was sure Madison couldn't perform any witchcraft against me, but Trent was still here.

"Good thing I'm not a witch." Trent licked his lips before baring his teeth. "I'll drain your blood and frame another vampire for the crime. Atlas would be a perfect choice. I've been dying to get rid of him."

In an instant, I grasped my locket. The night Trent attacked me, Luella appeared after I held my mother's necklace. Just as before, heat radiated up my arm and spread across my entire body. I prayed this meant it was working, but I wouldn't rely on Luella coming to my rescue. As I thought of ways to get away from Madison and Trent, I kept the locket in my hand.

"You were the one saying to make her death look like an accident. If you set up Atlas, the whole paranormal community will freak out," Madison said.

"So this is just a power grab for each of you? Trent can take over the vampires, and Madison can have the witches? I'm not dying for you two wannabe dictators." The minute I said that, I regretted it. Both of them turned red and yelled at me. I couldn't hear either of them as their voices grew louder and stronger. With no other choice, I ran toward the door I came in.

"Finally, I get fast food." Trent growled as he chased after me, with Madison trailing behind him.

Images of my mother and daughter flashed before my eyes as I ran. I wouldn't see Olivia again, which made me race forward. As Trent and Madison closed the gap, I grasped my necklace harder, making my hand hurt. But I didn't care. I had to find my inner witch and get myself out of this situation. An incantation came to me, and I shouted it at the top of my lungs.

"To my ancestors and my coven, my plea I share, guide my actions, keep me from despair. With courage and strength, in ways that are fair, defend me from evil, with love and care."

I didn't know how I knew it, but it didn't matter. Madison grasped her head and collapsed on the ground. She rolled into a ball and rocked back and forth.

I stopped yelling and stared at her. Causing anyone physical harm wasn't what our coven did or even what I normally would want to do. But then again, she wanted me dead.

"Madison, get up! Althea, stop whatever you did to her." Trent kicked her side. "Fine. I'll kill you both."

I repeated the incantation, hoping it would work on Trent, but he stormed over to me. My hand reached for the doorknob, but then the door opened.

"Trent, no!" Luella screamed as she stomped through the door. She pushed her hands forward in the air, and Trent collapsed on the ground. She hadn't even touched him.

"Althea Rose Fontenot, you just can't stay out of trouble, can you?"

39

———

Luella stepped aside as Evangeline rushed into the room. Evangeline wrapped her arms around me as I cried. Luella picked up Trent by the arms and legs and dragged him next to Madison. She dumped him on the ground. I really needed to find out how she became so strong, but that was for another day.

"Did you do that?" Luella asked.

She pointed at Madison, still moaning with her hands on her head.

"I did, but the spell didn't work on Trent."

Evangeline and I joined Luella. I was tempted to kick Trent to make myself feel better, but I knew it wouldn't. And I needed answers from him.

"You just need more practice. I'm glad you used your locket to call for help," Luella said.

"Thank you for finding me. I don't know what would've happened if you hadn't shown up," I said.

"Althea, you are a smart woman and a powerful witch. I have no doubt you would have figured a way out of your predicament." Luella placed her hand on my cheek. "You are not alone in this. Your coven is always here for you."

"What do we do now?" I asked.

"I had a coven member call Seraphine, since this is her warehouse, so we'll wait for her," Luella said. "Hopefully it won't take her long to get here."

"What is going on?" Seraphine Bordelon entered the room, eyes blazing and her hands in fists.

"Seraphine, you got here quickly," Luella said.

"I was close by, and when your witch said there was an issue at my warehouse, I ran." Seraphine walked up to Luella.

In those heels? I said to Evangeline, telepathically, of course. She nodded, keeping her eyes focused on Seraphine.

"You have proof Madison and Trent were responsible for Chloe's death?" Seraphine demanded.

"Yes, I do." I reached into my pocket and brought out my phone. "I recorded their conversation, including the part where they were deciding how to kill me."

Seraphine put her hand up to her red lips and stooped by Madison. "Can you stop this hex on her? She can't escape now."

"I don't know. The spell just came to me," I said.

"You did this?" Seraphine's disbelief came through loud and clear.

"Let me reverse it." Luella kneeled next to Madison and whispered in her ear. Madison stopped moaning and took her hands off her head. She lay on her back and stared upward.

Seraphine then stood up and faced me. "Your powers are strong, Althea."

I searched her face, looking for the compliment that

matched her voice. Instead, I found anger in her eyes. Was the anger for Madison for her actions, or for me?

"Althea did it to protect herself. We have no interest in harming another witch." Luella put her arm around me.

Seraphine lost the anger in her eyes and tears welled up. "I understand. It's so hard to believe young Madison would do this to anyone. Trent must have mesmerized her. She's so impressionable."

I slipped out of Luella's arm and crouched next to Madison. "Who decided to kill Chloe? Did you kill the other witches in our coven?"

Madison didn't move a muscle and stared up at the ceiling. I checked her pulse, so she was alive. While Madison was a killer, I didn't mean to harm her when I did the hex.

"She'll come out of it soon. Don't worry, Thea," Evangeline said.

The spell Luella used to stop Trent was still in effect. She stood by his feet and said, "Trent, you may speak now. Tell us the truth about Chloe's murder."

Trent attempted to shift his limbs, but an unseen force anchored him to the ground. "Let me up, you witches!"

Seraphine stood next to Luella. "Together, we can get him to talk. Should we try?" She bent over Trent and whispered in his ear. Luella grabbed her elbow and pulled her away from Trent.

"Seraphine, we should let the vampires handle Trent," Luella said.

"If you think so." Seraphine shook her arm out of Luella's grasp. "We must investigate if he is involved in a witch-killing conspiracy. Especially if Madison can't speak."

"She won't be able to talk?" My voice cracked.

Evangeline came up to me and squeezed my hand.

"We'll have to wait and see," Luella said.

"What about Trent?" I asked. "Knox told me they don't arrest vampires because they disappear."

"Atlas will handle it. He'll be here any moment," Luella said.

Atlas arrived through the back door after a minute of us staring at each other. I wanted to call his name, but I let him be. He was a vampire on a mission.

"Trent, you will be brought up to the council at once." A vein pulsed in Atlas's neck.

"I'm sorry, Atlas," Luella said softly.

"I am, too. He's always been a handful, but I never imagined he would turn his back on the paranormal community." Atlas stared at Trent, his anger mixed with sadness.

"We need to find out what he knows about Madison's plans. Who else is involved, Trent?" Luella demanded.

"I'll never tell! The Fontenot Coven is doomed!" Trent screamed.

"Luella, can you release Trent so I may take him?" Atlas asked.

As she did with Madison, she whispered in Trent's ear. She backed away from him and Atlas took her place. I expected Trent to run, but he didn't move a muscle. His bravado disappeared as Atlas stood over him. He cowered when Atlas grabbed him by the arm and pulled up to his feet. Trent's feet and wrists seemed as if they were tightly bound. Vampires had more powers than I realized. Or maybe it was just Atlas.

"You'll let us know what you learn?" Seraphine placed her hands on Atlas' arm.

"Yes, and you will do the same about Madison." Atlas' voice was firm, and Seraphine blinked a few times as he spoke, but she nodded.

"Althea, I'm sorry." The pain on Atlas's face matched his

voice. Before I could respond, he returned to a shivering Trent and grabbed him fiercely by the wrists. A cloud of fog surrounded them as they turned into bats. Trent's pleas faded as they disappeared through the open door and into the star-dotted sky.

40

As if on cue, the next paranormal entered the warehouse. Knox, dressed in a suit instead of his Mardi Gras costume, barged through the door. A smudge of silver paint remained on his chin, but I didn't dare tell him. By his glowing eyes and flared nostrils, I worried he was going to shift into a werewolf.

He didn't, but he was a furious detective.

"Tell me what is going on here." Knox tromped over to Luella. "Miss Lulu, I got your message, and I'll give you five minutes before I call in reinforcements."

"Althea, perhaps you would like to explain?" Luella turned her head toward me.

No, I didn't want to explain. I wanted to go home and eat ice cream and forget all this happened. But I had no choice. I took in a deep breath and recounted what happened with Madison and Trent. Knox didn't interrupt me, but checked on Madison while I spoke. She still didn't move or speak.

"Well, that's quite the story, Althea." Knox shook his head. "Don't worry, I believe you, but I am glad you recorded the conversation. Of course, we won't be able to arrest Trent."

"Atlas took him," Luella said.

"I don't know what the vampire council will do with him, but I imagine it's worse than jail," Knox said.

I hated to admit it, but that thought made me happy for a split second. Trent didn't deserve my sympathy, but wanting someone to suffer wasn't part of my DNA. Which was why every time I looked at Madison, a sinking feeling came over me. She was so young, and I hadn't meant to hurt her. But then again, she wanted to kill me.

"All right. Before I call this in, let us get a few things straight. Say nothing about witchcraft or vampires. Just tell the truth, but avoid talking about spells or suspects becoming bats and flying away. Do y'all understand?"

Luella, Evangeline, and I, said, "Yes."

"Seraphine? Do you agree?" Knox walked next to her. She was kneeling beside Madison, holding her hand.

"Sorry, yes, I do. We'll have to say Madison suffered a seizure. The doctors will probably see it that way." Seraphine stood up. "I'd like to go with her to the hospital. Although she is a murderess, she was a member of my family's coven, and I am responsible for her."

"That won't be a problem. I'm going to make that call now. Stay put and don't touch anything." Knox walked away from us and took out his cell phone.

"I meant what I said, Luella. I am responsible for Madison, and I apologize for her actions." Seraphine focused on Madison and didn't look at Luella. "Once she can speak, I'll find out why she did this."

"Thank you. I hope this is the end of this situation." The icy stare she gave to the back of Seraphine's head seemed to show that Luella didn't believe this was the end. Unfortunately, I agreed.

Finally, at 2:00 a.m., a police officer drove Luella, Evangeline, and I back to Fontenot Mansion. We went to the table by the fountain in the courtyard.

"Give me light on this dark night," Evangeline said, and the candles on the table lit themselves.

Although I was exhausted, I giggled. "Magic really has some excellent uses."

Luella lowered herself into a chair as if she had aged twenty years.

"You must be drained from the spell you put on Trent." Evangeline sat next to Luella and put her hand on hers.

"Taking down that bat was easy," Luella said with a small smile, but then frowned. "I am concerned about Madison."

"Honestly, I don't understand how I did that to her." I slumped into the chair on the other side of Luella. "Do you think she'll come out of that coma, or whatever it is?"

"Only if Seraphine lets her," Luella said.

"What?" Evangeline and I said in unison.

"I hate to say this since Seraphine and I have had a rapport since she took over her coven"—Luella wiped a tear from her face—"but Madison couldn't have pulled off the murders of four witches on her own, even with Trent's help. She had help from a more experienced witch."

"You think Seraphine did this?" Evangeline gasped. "But why?"

"I hope it isn't her, but someone is trying to take our power away from us," Luella said. "Madison and Trent killed Chloe, but we have no proof they killed our other witches."

"Including my mother." I stood up from my chair and sat on the edge of the fountain. The cold water numbed my fingers as I swirled them around. My heart wasn't numb to the pain of not knowing who killed my mother.

"We need answers to many things, but hopefully, Knox will have some of them." Luella flicked her wrist, and I heard the courtyard gate open up.

"I thought y'all might still be up," he said.

"Take a seat, Knox. You've had quite the evening," Luella said.

"I would, but I need to go to the hospital. No, Madison's condition hasn't changed." Knox put up his hand to stop us from asking. "I wanted to tell you we didn't find Chloe's locket anywhere in the warehouse or her apartment."

"Thank you. I appreciate you looking for it." Luella didn't look surprised by this information.

"You're welcome. I also came to let Althea know she is not a person of interest any longer, so she's free to go." Knox sat next to me on the edge of the fountain. "But let me tell you what I always tell my sister, Cricket. Don't go kicking fresh dung on a hot day."

"Is that a werewolf saying?" I shook my head.

Knox grinned. "No, it's for everyone. It means don't go looking for trouble. I hope you'll be part of our community without the drama."

He stood up and offered his hand. I shook it and said, "Thanks for your help, Knox. I'm sorry to ruin your Mardi Gras parade."

Knox shrugged as he walked toward the exit. "Oh, it wasn't the first one ruined, and I'm sure it won't be the last. Just don't let it be you again."

His laughter trailed off until the gate banged closed.

"Knox is a hoot sometimes," Evangeline said. "I wish he had found the locket, though."

"I've called for Atlas, so perhaps he'll know about it," Luella said. "Here he is now."

A bat glided into the courtyard and a cloud of smoke formed. Atlas, the man, or rather, a vampire, appeared next to Luella.

"I received your message, Luella. Is everyone all right?" Atlas asked.

It took every ounce of restraint not to throw my arms around Atlas. The sadness in his eyes broke my heart.

"We're as good as we can be. Knox was just here and said Madison is still the same." Luella stood up and gave Atlas the hug I wanted to give him. Well, mine wouldn't have been as motherly as hers. "How are you?"

"The same as you. Trent's actions shouldn't surprise me, but..." Atlas shook his head.

"Betrayal hurts no matter who it is," Evangeline said.

"Well said, Evangeline." Atlas reached into his pocket. "I found this among Trent's possessions and wanted to return it to your coven. I didn't find any other lockets."

He gave the locket to Luella. We watched as Evangeline turned it over to reveal the last name Chase. The locket belonged to Chloe. There was still one missing.

"We appreciate having this back." Luella clasped the locket in her hand and raised it to her heart.

"The council extends their apologies for Trent's actions. He will pay for his crimes in our court system. You have my word," Atlas said.

"Thank you for everything. We owe you a debt of gratitude," Luella said.

"There is no scoreboard. We all help when it's right, no

matter the cost." Atlas pain was too much to bear. I walked back to the fountain and turned around to wipe my tears.

"Althea." Atlas was now next to me, his hand on my shoulder.

"Yes?" I turned to face him.

"Your empathy is palpable. Please do not worry about me." He smiled sadly. "I am used to loss. You don't need to concern yourself with my feelings."

"I can't help it." I returned his smile. "When my family and friends are in pain, I worry."

"That's what makes you a good person and a good witch." He leaned down and kissed me on the cheek. "I am honored to be your friend."

Before I could react or say a word, Atlas turned into a bat and flew toward the moon. No man ever turned into a bat after kissing me. But then again, that wasn't the strangest thing that had happened this week.

"I tell you what, that bat sure can make an exit."

I looked down at where Tasso brushed up against my legs.

"And you know how to make an entrance. I'm so happy to see you." I picked Tasso up and buried my face in his fur.

"Cher, don't you cry." Tasso licked the tears that fell down my face.

I returned to the table with Tasso in my arms. Evangeline and Luella were crying, too.

"Look at us witches crying like babies." Evangeline laughed after we wiped our tears. "We needed that, though."

"I think we need something else, too." I put Tasso and the table. "Let me give this new spell a try."

I pushed my chair back and opened my arms, as if waiting for something. "In weariness, our bodies and souls are mired. Please nourish our spirits and bodies as we desire."

A pint of Rocky Road ice cream appeared in my hands. Luella had a bowl of banana pudding with vanilla wafers on top, and Evangeline had a plate of beignets. Tasso had a bowl of seafood gumbo.

"Look at you! You're back to your old tricks, my friend!" Evangeline squealed and picked up a beignet. "Oh, it's so warm!"

"So is my gumbo. Thank you kindly, Thea-Bea." Tasso slurped his gumbo, letting it stain the fur around his mouth.

Luella didn't touch her pudding but reached over and held my hand. "You did well today, Althea Rose. But I need to tell you one thing."

"Yes, ma'am?" I faced her, bracing for a reprimand.

"Remember, you can't date a vampire, no matter how attractive or kind he is."

"Luella, I told you I'm not here for a vacation romance." I sighed.

"Oh, honey, you're not here on a vacation. You're home now, aren't you?"

I squeezed Luella's hand before I let it go. "Fontenot Mansion is home for now. There is still work to be done."

There were still many questions to be answered. I needed to find out who killed my mother and the other witches in our coven. If Seraphine Bordelon and her coven were involved, we had to find out. And I still was in the dark about the ritual that caused her to leave here and block my magic and memories. I also had promised to help Evangeline with her husband's disappearance.

"Of course she's staying!" Tasso licked his lips and jumped off the table. "I tell you what, Thea-Bea, you brought just what this coven needed."

"And what's that?" I asked.

"Strength, determination, and a lot of heart. Welcome home." Tasso meowed, then jumped on the courtyard wall and disappeared on the other side.

Fontenot Mansion was my home until I found all my answers. After that, I didn't know what I would do. For the time being, I planned to enjoy my new family and world. I didn't need magic to know I had to be here.

Althea's journey in New Orleans continues with
Red Beans and Rituals.

To keep up on my new releases,
join my newsletter at www.jenpittsauthor.com

ACKNOWLEDGMENTS

I fell in love with New Orleans and vampires the first time I read Anne Rice's *Interview with the Vampire*. My love of the city and witches continued with her book *The Witching Hour*. Anne Rice deeply affected my life as a person and writer.

My husband's unwavering support of my work and everything else in my life means the world. I love you.

My children are used to my strange conversations about mysteries, New Orleans, and now the paranormal. Thank you for understanding and loving your momma no matter what I talk about.

Thanks to my cats, Mabel, and Dipper, for keeping me company as I write. I promise one day I'll have a book about you two.

Once again, a huge thank you to Dad and Wanda. You keep reading and supporting my work and it means the world. I love y'all.

My critique group and the BARN Writers Studio have been with me from the beginning and I'm thankful y'all are still here.

A huge thank you to the most amazing beta-readers: Chrystal, Jenna, Katy, Lynn, Leann, Wanda, and Dad. Your advice, support, and encouragement make me a better writer.

Thanks to my new editor, Paula, for joining me on this

new cozy paranormal journey. I'm glad to have you as part of my writing team.

Authors write alone, but we don't work alone. I am thankful for the community of cozy mystery writers across the world. The interactions, whether online, on Zoom, or even in person, make this amazing profession even more fun. A special thanks to Lynn for introducing me to so many writers and for helping me with this book and so much more. Thanks also to Eryn! She is my go-to for coffee-shop-hopping and an immense help and inspiration for my books. Y'all are the best!

Thank you to my family, friends, and readers for being here for me and my books! Thank you for joining me in this new world of paranormal cozies!

ABOUT THE AUTHOR

Jen Pitts is a lifelong mystery reader who turned her obsession into writing cozy mysteries of her own. When she isn't plotting fictional murder, she's chugging coffee, traveling, reading, and enjoying life with her husband, children, and two cats in the Pacific Northwest.

Learn more about Jen through her newsletter. A free short story prequel is available exclusively for newsletter members. Sign up at www.jenpittsauthor.com

And keep up daily with Jen on Facebook where she shares her books, her cats, and her love of New Orleans.

You can also find Jen on the following social media sites:

facebook.com/jenpittsmysteryauthor

instagram.com/jenpittsmysterywriter

goodreads.com/jenpitts

amazon.com/author/jenpitts

bookbub.com/authors/jen-pitts

ALSO BY JEN PITTS

The French Quarter Mystery Series:

Coffee, a Scone, and a Place to Call Home - a Short Story Prequel

The Key to Murder

The Gates to the Afterlife

A Deadly Check-In

Bury the Past

The Dead End Tour

A Corpse in the Cafe

The Witches of the French Quarter Series:

Mardi Gras and Magic

Red Beans and Rituals